I0656981

Charles Clarke

The Beauclercs

Father and son: Vol. I.

Charles Clarke

The Beauclercs
Father and son: Vol. I.

ISBN/EAN: 9783337041182

Printed in Europe, USA, Canada, Australia, Japan

Cover: Foto ©Andreas Hilbeck / pixelio.de

More available books at **www.hansebooks.com**

THE BEAUCLERCS

FATHER AND SON.

A Novel.

BY

CHARLES CLARKE,

AUTHOR OF "CHARLIE THORNHILL," "WHICH IS THE WINNER," &c. &c.

IN THREE VOLUMES.

VOL. I.

LONDON:

CHAPMAN AND HALL, 193, PICCADILLY.

1867.

LONDON:
PRINTED BY C. WHITING, BEAUFORT HOUSE, STRAND.

CONTENTS OF VOL. I.

CHAPTER I.

EARLY PATRONAGE 1   PAGE

CHAPTER II.

NAVAL ENGAGEMENT 17

CHAPTER III.

THE COLVILLES OF LYMMERSFIELD 40

CHAPTER IV.

MOTHERLESS CHILDREN 55

CHAPTER V.

MADAME ROSENFELS 73

CHAPTER VI.

FRANK BECOMES A MAN 89

CHAPTER VII.

A REAL WOMAN 119

CHAPTER VIII.
                                                  PAGE
A New Acquaintance   142

CHAPTER IX.
A Pic-nic 163

CHAPTER X.
The Boating Party 185

CHAPTER XI.
Violet's Trustees 196

CHAPTER XII.
Our Village 214

CHAPTER XIII.
Just Joined 231

CHAPTER XIV.
A Transplantation 261

THE BEAUCLERCS, FATHER AND SON.

CHAPTER I.

EARLY PATRONAGE.

——consuefacere filium
Suâ sponte rectè facere, quam alieno metu.
Hoc Pater ac Dominus interest.

TERENCE'S *Adelphi.*

"WHO's that, Dobbs, in the well-made trousers and tight jacket?"

"Young Beauclerc, a lower-form boy: he came this half," said Dobbs, in reply to his friend Carloss's inquiry.

"Whose house is he in?"

"Purser's, I believe; looks sharp set, doesn't he?"

"No; I don't see it, Dobbs; he's a deuced neat little fellow; by Jove, how well his jacket fits

VOL. I.   B

him! Young swell, I should think, by the look of him," added Carloss; "I'm going to make his acquaintance."

"How do you propose to do that?" inquired Dobson, who was prepared for some eccentricity, from his knowledge of his companion.

"You'll see. Hallo! you fellow, Beauclerc!" The little fellow turned round, and disclosed a face quite in keeping with the smartness of his figure. "Come here a moment."

Beauclerc came towards the two boys, looking fearlessly up in their faces; he had hardly had time to realise the profound dignity of a sixth-form boy, or he might have looked more abashed.

"What form are you in?" said Carloss.

"The shell," said the little fellow, cheerfully and undauntedly.

"Where were you before you came here?" inquired his interrogator.

"Nowhere at all," said he, understanding the question to apply to school.

"Was it a nice place?"

The boy laughed, and showed dimples that are only becoming to women and schoolboys.

"How often did they flog there?" No answer.

" Come, out with it, like a man. Twice a week ? or only every Monday prospectively ? "

" I was at a private tutor's." And as he drew up his neat little figure and handsome face it was quite clear that he meant to impress his auditors with a sense of the superiority of that system of education.

" Oh ! really ; I know the system," said Dobson, who had himself enjoyed the fullest gratification, as a youngster, of thick bread-and-butter, resurrection pies, and corporal punishment at a county grammar school : " Turkey carpets, patent leather boots at tea-time, change of socks after exercise, treacle posset, and modern languages. And where was that, my boy ? "

" That was at Mr. Colville's, at Lymmersfield."

Carloss turned quickly round from something which had attracted his attention for a moment, and said,

" Colville's, were you at Colville's ? What sort of a fellow is he ? "

" Capital, and so is his wife," said the boy, eagerly.

" I should think you were a judge," observed the other, laughing. " Did you ever see my little sister Violet there?" added he, at the same time.

"No; never: but I heard of her having been there once when I was away."

"I'm glad of that, for you'd have been dangerous to her peace of mind." The boy looked up smilingly at Carloss, not knowing exactly what to make of him. "Do you ever fag, Beauclerc?"

"Sometimes."

"In those neat-looking gloves, I hope?" said Carloss, good-humouredly.

"Not when I have to fetch the butter for Dorrien's tea."

"No, I should think not: keep them for blacking boots. However, take them off now, and run down to Dripping's as fast as you can. Ask him for a quarter of a pound of butter, two Yarmouth bloaters, four French rolls, and a pound of sugar for Carloss, and bring them up to my study." The little fellow was just starting, when he was stopped again. "And I say, young 'un, bring your verse-task for to-morrow, and I'll do it for you."

Beauclerc departed on his errand, a common one enough in those days with every lower-form boy in a public school, and conveying to the mind no degradation whatever. Everybody had gone through it, and it was as natural to a schoolboy as a kilt to a Highlander.

The two elder boys, Dobson and Carloss, strolled away from the top of the school lane, where this conversation had taken place, and bent their steps towards the country, intent upon a walk, before their anticipated rolls and bloaters.

" What in the world did you mean by your little sister, Carloss ? I thought you were the last hope of the descendants of John of Gaunt ? "

This was a joke at the school-house; but as Carloss believed in it he always took it *au sérieux.*

" I've no doubt I was the last hope, for you know my governor was not in a position to provide such luxuries as descendants for the family : his elder brother's business, Dobbs. However, hope is delusive, *spes fallax,* and about six years after my birth came my little sister Violet." Dobbs seemed tired of the conversation, feeling no great interest in girls in general, nor Carloss's sister in particular ; so he turned it into his own channel.

" I wonder you don't work, old fellow," said he, looking into Carloss's face with more curiosity perhaps than affection. Dobson affected highlows, rather short trousers, and hair which was constantly falling over his forehead and eyes, and being pushed off again by well-inked fingers.

"What's the use of it?" replied the other, who was as great a contrast to his companion as can well be imagined. "*Cui bono?* as you swells have it."

"Why, if only to leave in the sixth; it would be so jolly." The sixth was Dobson's seventh heaven, as near it as could be: and a gulf of immeasurable depth separated it from the rest of the world. Even talking to his friend Carloss, he felt something like an angel of light with a deep regret for Satan's misfortunes. Carloss was only in the upper fifth.

"Ah! that's it, exactly," said Carloss, "to leave in the sixth! that strikes me as absurd. If I was going to stay in the sixth, like you, Dobbs, why, perhaps it would be worth while; but I think I shall do for the riding-school by Easter."

"Yes, old fellow, I know that; but just to have got your remove this last quarter; and you could do it so easily. Old Armstrong would be so pleased. You're rather a favourite of his."

"What! because I won the long jump. Well, he's a good fellow; but I don't think I can oblige him in this particular. Slaughtering Frenchmen is a much higher ambition than writing sapphics."

"It's a pity you should be thrown away upon the army; why don't you go to Oxford, and then to the bar? that's what I shall do. Then I shall try to get into Parliament, and——"

"Then you'll slaughter your thousands too; only it will be with a jaw-bone; you know the animal, Dobbs."

"Not so bad, 'pon my soul!" said Dobbs, as he attempted feebly to bonnet his friend.

As they returned by the meadows, alongside of the river, to school, they remarked that it had risen remarkably within the last hour or two.

"That's the snow from the Welsh hills: it goes down as rapidly, though, as it rises."

"I don't know about that. I remember once all the lower part of the town being flooded, and the people going about in punts."

"Splendid fun!" said Carloss.

"I don't know about that, either: there was no end of property destroyed, and the lower floors of all the houses were under water for three days. I remember it; I was flogged for being nearly drowned."

"What an odd punishment for such a diversion."

"Oh! it was my fault," said Dobson, who, having enshrined Dr. Armstrong, felt no compunction at any form or extent of worship. "It was all right. He said he'd flog any fellow that got wet through again by going into the streets in a boat. I did get wet through, body and soul; and it took three-quarters of an hour before I was brought to; and the next day I got six cuts."

"Going about in boats in the street; by Jove! that would be a lark." And having arrived at this conclusion and at the school at the same time, Carloss said no more.

Meantime Frank Beauclerc had been to Mr. Dripping, and had returned with an armful of rolls and sugar, and hands-full of butter and bloaters: and having deposited them on one of the study tables, waited patiently the return of the proprietor. The studies at Dr. Armstrong's were comfortable rooms enough; and while they answered their purpose of patent digesters for mental aliment, they were no less useful for recruiting the forces of the

body, when a more than ordinary share of repose
and comfort was required. Each study was a
square and lofty apartment of about fourteen or
fifteen feet. It contained two green baize-covered
tables, at each end of which was a drawer. There
were four rush-bottomed chairs; two bookcases,
divided equally into two parts; a coal-box, shovel,
poker, and tongs: and that these latter might not
lack exercise, there was a fireplace of but moderate dimensions. To be sure, as it chiefly served
for mulling in small quantities the smaller beer
which was smuggled from the hall dinner, and for
grilling cold meat, the necessity for increasing its
dimensions was not so apparent as if its primary
use had been for heating whole bodies. The rooms
looked on to a cheerful court, whence might be
seen objects of considerable interest, but not in
great numbers: occasional maid-servants, with or
without children, to and fro between the masters'
houses and the street; little boys going and coming
on some such errands as Frank Beauclerc's, laden
with tarts, butter, eggs, ham, and sugar; big boys
lounging in the doorways, or amusing themselves
before the ground-floor windows, sometimes with
fencing-foils or boxing-gloves, and at certain times

with heavy books, preparing the final polish for an afternoon construe, before appearing in the presence of the Doctor. Regularly, too, at twelve o'clock, might be seen the second master, who lived in the house which occupied the third side of the court, escorting his wife on their daily constitutional. And a remarkably pretty woman she was; so much so, that Dobson himself was induced to leave that interesting chorus in the Frogs of Aristophanes, beginning with,

$$\text{Βρεκεκεκὲξ κοάξ κοάξ,}$$
$$\text{Βρεκεκεκὲξ κοάξ κοάξ,}$$

whenever he heard a shout from some less ardent admirer of the Greek comedian of "Here comes old Swipes and his wife!"

The sounds, too, which issued from the study-windows were suggestive of uncultivated talent. "My Love is like the red, red rose," on a flute, purchased second-hand at a bookstall; "Auld Robin Gray," and "The Lass of Richmond Hill," set as an accompaniment, but played without it, on the cornet-à-piston; a nigger melody on the banjo; and the intermingled yells of a junior, sentenced by a court scholastic to a dozen from the prepositors for breach of discipline, loaded the air, like a Dutch concert, not unfrequently more in rivalry than in unison.

In such a room stood Frank Beauclerc. He had had time to notice a dog-whip, a leaded stick for the destruction of game, a half-finished net, a blacking-pot and pair of brushes, and a kettle, when Carloss and Dobson entered.

" Now, young 'un, out with the teapot, and put the kettle on the fire; there, that will do. Now while the tea brews bring us your verses." Beauclerc hesitated.

" What are they ? "

" Bland," said the boy.

" Well, then, go and fetch them." The boy stood still. " Why, you young vagabond ! I do believe he doubts our capacity, Dobbs."

" Ah! that's because you are not in the sixth; now then, be off."

Beauclerc, thus adjured, went out, and returned, bringing a copy of Bland's verses, and a sheet of paper, rather the worse for his experiments.

" Here, give us hold," said Carloss, snatching the book and the paper; " how many ?"

" Six ; for to-morrow, at second lesson.   I shall
have time to do them."

" Nonsense ; I know Bland by heart.   Toast
that herring ; and if you burn it, Dobbs will be
down upon you.   Where do you begin ? "

" But——" began Frank again, and then stopped
and blushed, evidently anxious to say something,
but afraid.

" Well ! what is it ? "

" I think I'd better do them myself ; I really
am much obliged——"

" So I should think, if you're going to do them
all like this.   Why, here are false quantities enough
in these two lines to get the whole of the shell sent
down !   Don't you know that the first o in novo
is short, and that you can't have a word of three
syllables at the end of a short line.   I hope your
friend Colville didn't tell you that you might ? "

" No ! I knew it was wrong, but I couldn't do
it any other way."

" Then, look here ; that is the way to do the
line.'   And Carloss wrote the two lines as they
should be.

" But I'd rather try to do them myself," said the

boy, at last, colouring as he spoke, but looking his patron in the face.

" But suppose you can't ? "

" Mr. Colville told me always to do my own work."

" Very right," said Dobbs. " Did he tell you why ? "

" He said it was deceiving my master not to do so ? "

" Dobbs, that's a phenomenon. What else did he say ? "

" That if I did that, and never told a lie, Dr. Armstrong would never flog me."

" Did he ? Perhaps he was right," said the other; " though it never struck me in that light. At all events, he was a gentleman."

" So he was, I'm sure," replied Frank, making the most of his opportunity. " So if you'll give me the paper, I'll try to do them myself."

" Let him have them, Carloss. There, sit down there, and turn them into Latin, and we'll help you when you are hard up. Hollo! mind the bloaters, you've upset the shovel. You're a lucky fellow to have begun life under a gentleman, and to have come here afterwards. I wish I had. The first time I ever told the truth I was flogged for it, I remember; and it made a great impression."

" Did it? Is there any more cream?" inquired Reginald Carloss.

" Yes; they couldn't find out who cut down a gooseberry-tree in the playground, and I said that I did. The master called the confession gross insolence, and flogged me before the whole school; so I never told the truth again until I came here."

By-and-by the verses were done, and the tea and bloaters were eaten, and Beauclerc was going away, delighted with his new patrons.

" Stop a moment," said Dobbs, who saw a fine opportunity for airing his professional talents; so Frank stopped, and looked down. " Do you ever analyse motives?" And Dobson put his hands deep in his pockets, and his head on one side, and looked as like an Old Bailey counsel as possible.

" Hang it, Dobbs, don't tease the boy; what the deuce should he know about analysing motives?"

" Wait a moment, O descendant of kings. Do you ever analyse motives?"

" I don't know what you mean," said the fag, in

a mild tone of voice, and looking down at his boots, instead of up, as a witness should look.

"Well, come now, witness, I mean, Beauclerc, do you tell the truth because it's right to do so, or because old Colville, or whatever his name is, told you that Dr. Armstrong wouldn't flog you?" And here Dobson looked as important as possible for a barrister without his wig and gown. "Now, take time."

And indeed the witness, as he was called, seemed very likely to obey this latter mandate by not answering at all. He only blushed and looked again at his boots, which were not so clean as before his walk to Dripping's.

"Don't bother the boy," said Carloss.

"You've no taste for analysis of character," said Dobson, "and never will have, while you remain in the fifth form. Let me recommend the Ethics of the mighty Stagyrite to your notice. Come, young man, you're on your oath. Why do you tell the truth? Which is the motive?"

"Because Dr. Armstrong would flog me if I didn't."

"There," said Dobbs, triumphantly, "that's a most extraordinary phase of the contradictions of

character. By the answer he's given, which is
symbolical of truth in the highest degree, he
proves that he doesn't lie, only from a most
unworthy motive—physical fear. Now you may
go." And as Beauclerc made off, verse-task in
hand, Dobbs's delight was so great that he threw
a book which he held in his hand after him.
"There, old fellow, what do you think of that for
an examination of an unwilling witness?"

"Dobbs, you're a lunatic; there goes the
prayer-bell."

CHAPTER II.

A NAVAL ENGAGEMENT.

Quid juvat errores mersâ jam puppe fateri?

So Frank Beauclerc began his public school days. Nor must these early chapters of his boyhood be regarded as a work of supererogation by those who long to plunge into the middle of affairs at once, or who look for a ghost, a murder, or a trial for bigamy, thus early in the story of his life. The careful development of character, and the steps by which our hero climbs to distinction, good or bad, are the peculiar duties of the conscientious novelist. One knows what a goodsized insect is without the use of the microscope, but not without some detailed examination of his parts.

It was a great thing for a lower-form boy to have dropped upon his feet so dexterously in a large public school like Dr. Armstrong's, and that by his own merits. Not that he got his lessons or verses done by the " big fellows; " not at all, he would not submit to such a degradation. The Beauclercs, though an easy-going lot, were blessed with a proper pride. But he got just that amount of help from those who were able to give it, which does so much to encourage and to inform younger boys. In private schools they ought to get it from their masters, in public schools they do get it from the boys. It only requires a discriminating self-dependence not to claim too much nor too frequently.

Then this patronage extended itself to all games, in which he became an adept above his fellows, and sometimes to scrapes which were not so good for him, out of which, however, he was taught to walk like a gentleman, after having run into them like a schoolboy. The truthfulness of his character made him popular with the good fellows, and obtained for him a certain respect with the bad; and long after his friends Dobson and Carloss had gone, the one to Oxford, the other to the sanguinary service in which his soul delighted, their influence was felt by their *protégé*.

There was another bond of union between this little fellow and his very dashing schoolfellow, Carloss. They were both Indian, before the miscellaneous body who could pass a good examination, and wanted a provision for life or death, had sounded the tocsin in Bengal, Madras, or Bombay. The Beauclercs and Carlosses dated from Clive's days, and the boys for four generations had only been sent home to be sent back again at an age when they could appreciate the good things which were in store for them. Every house in Calcutta was open to such names as these, as to their fathers before them. Not so to the Joneses and Smiths, who had satisfied the Civil Service examiners of their capacity, but whose characters and respectability remained to be proved before a naturally prejudiced tribunal. The Beauclercs and the Carlosses declared it was all over with India, and prepared to come home as soon as their circumstances would let them.

The Saber did not overflow its banks this time, to the present disappointment of Carloss. His eminently practical mind—regardless of possible

consequences to the dwellers in the Low Cut, near
the Alderman's Bridge, Grammerton—had fore-
seen and longed for the certain pleasures of a
punting party, and, in the absence of his favourite
arm of the service, cavalry, a naval engagement.
The melting process in the Welsh hills was slower
than usual, and gave room for the body of water
to get away with nothing more important than a
few odd shirts and chemises, happening to be on
the hedges, "which it was a fine day," as Mrs.
Soaper remarked, when requested by the owners to
account for their disappearance.

Beauclerc passed much of his time in Carloss's
study, where he was sometimes fagged, sometimes licked, and sometimes taught. He impli-
citly believed that it was all for his good. A
great deal of it was so.

"Come here, Frank: who was that fellow I
saw you with yesterday evening, just before we
were gated?"

"Michaelson," said Frank, in a subdued tone.

"Didn't I tell you not to go about with Michaelson?"

"Yes." And the youngster began wondering
how many cuts the confession was worth.

" Why ?"

" Because you said he was a snob and a black-guard."

" Then what the d—— do you mean by being seen with him ?"

" I can't help it always; he's in our house; and besides, he can't help being poor and having no tin."

" I don't care about his tin; it isn't that. I tell you he's a bad lot. He's borrowed money of you, hasn't he ?"

Beauclerc would not answer.

" Tell me directly, Frank."

Still the boy was silent.

" How much was it? Now if you don't tell me the truth I'll break every bone in your body."

This ogre-like language is a true expression of scholastic friendship, and must not deter mothers from trusting their boys to the billows of the sea of troubles in a public school.

" Half a sovereign." And Beauclerc hung his head at speaking the truth.

" Half a sovereign? Why, you young million-naire, what the d—— do you mean by having half a sovereign? Have you got any more?"

" No; not till Easter."

" Has he paid you?"

" No; but I know he will when—when he can."

" Has he paid you any?"

" Not yet."

Carloss put his hand in his pocket, and, drawing out the money, placed it on the table before the boy. " There, take it up."

" Oh, Carloss! indeed, indeed, I can't; you're always so kind, but——"

" Will you take that money? You needn't be shy about it, for I'm going to commit an assault worth five sovereigns; I'm going to thrash you most heartily, and then I'm going to do the same by Michaelson." Saying which he thrust the money into his hand, while poor Frank's eyes filled with tears, and Carloss fulfilled to the letter his promises. " Now be off, and send Michaelson here directly."

Fortune favours the brave not unfrequently at the expense of other people. So this winter was a long one, and towards the end of it came more snow on the Welsh hills, and then a warm sun, and then the river rose. One night all Grammerton retired to bed; the western hills of Wales

were clothed in floods of rosy light at sunset, after
a cloudless day as little like winter as possible.
The next morning the water was in the cellars
of the Low Cut, and before breakfast it was near
choking the arches of the Alderman's Bridge
(flattering memorial of civic liberality), and chairs
and tables were being hauled up, high and dry,
through the windows; and cribs without their
tenants, and tenants without their cribs, and
rashers of bacon, alive and dead; and the poor
were opening their houses to those who had been
summarily ejected, as indeed I find they generally
do. And along the stream were the wharfingers
and boatmen securing their craft, and manufacturers moving their bales of flannel and woollen
goods, these descendants of the old Flemings, to
higher stories of the warehouses; and in the midst
of all this needless terror, but actual inconvenience
—you will hardly believe it!—those young rascals
at the schools were chuckling and rubbing their
hands in anticipation of a naval engagement in
the middle of the streets. What makes it more
important to us is that Carloss, who ought to have
known better, was at the head of them.

Dr. Armstrong was one of those admirable

schoolmasters that must necessarily be rare articles in any age. Time and space are not wasted in giving a few words to himself and his system. He was in himself a grand and noble gentleman, fitted to fill with respect, affection, or awe, the rising generation of the upper and middle classes of a country like this. A liberal, but no pedantic, admirer of classical literature, of accurate but very extensive reading among the ancients, and making this knowledge subservient to the other purposes of a practical life : interesting his pupils by the varied stories of apt illustration which he brought to bear upon their immediate pursuits. Withal a Christian gentleman of generous sentiments, conscious of his own powers, and not intolerant of the mistakes of other men. Need I say, after this, that he was large of frame, handsome of person, and clean shorn ?

Of the upper boys he made friends. His whole dependence was upon them for example and influence ; and he expected that like the barons of old they should be the transmitters (the μεσῖται) of all that was good in the governing body. Of the little boys he made pets. He liked to see them hearty in play, and energetic in and out of school.

But there was another class of schoolboy, usually at a discount with schoolmasters. I mean those boys whom physical courage and a sort of natural restlessness make impatient learners, but very excellent playmates. He regarded these as a sort of connecting link between the aristocracy of learning and the democratic mixture of talent, dirt, simplicity, idleness, and genuine boyhood. He tried to bring the playfulness of the schoolroom into his sixth form, and to carry down some of their dignity below. Some of them were idle; he knew that they wanted rousing. Some were stupid; they wanted enlightening. "The sixth may be trusted to go alone," said he, "and the little ones will have plenty of friends among the big ones; but who is to take care of the fellows who can only run and jump, and play football and cricket? That won't get them through such a world of scrambling and competition. I must look after them myself." So Reginald Carloss became a prime favourite with the Doctor, being remarkably sharp, but with no capability for reading.

"Oh, Carloss, I wish you'd do me a favour," said Frank Beauclerc, after second school one morning.

" What is it, young fellow; give you a construe ?"

" No, thank you; but let me go with you to the
punting match this afternoon."

" And who told you there was going to be a
punting match ?"

" I heard Digby tell one of the fellows in school
that he was going in Tremayne's boat as his squire,
and that you were going in another. I should so
like to see it."

" You'll be flogged if you're found out, Master
Frank, so I tell you; and what will your friend
Colville say ?"

" I don't think he'd mind, if he knew it wasn't
for lying or lessons. The only things he cares
about are falsehoods and false quantities. He says
they're both the signs of a depraved mind."

" Oh, I suppose he sees some connexion between
them. Everybody is born with a depraved mind
then, for nobody ever wrote Latin verse by instinct:
at least I never saw him. So you'll run the chance
of a flogging ?"

" He won't flog *me*. What would he do if he
was to catch *you* ?"

"Set me a book of Homer: and make me do it, too."

"That's awkward." And Frank Beauclerc began to think the expedition would be given up. He was soon undeceived.

"Well! it would be, just now. For do you know, Frank, I've been gazetted to the —— Hussars, and am ordered to join on Friday, which is impossible if I don't start to-morrow." Poor Frank was so shocked by this intelligence that he felt half inclined to cry. Nothing but the prospect of the naval engagement prevented his tears; "You shall go, Beauclerc, but hold your tongue about it."

The longest time between callings-over was from three to five; and the shortest road to the lower end of Grammerton was by some meadows at the back of the school fields. By five minutes after three there were twenty-four schoolboys, all anxious to be punted from one street to another, and apparently willing to pay any money or promise anything for a privilege which the rest of the inhabitants only seemed anxious to avoid. While they bargain with Peter the boatman and his satel-

lites for his punts, we will just give a short description of Grammerton itself, which may account for
the peculiarity of its present necessities.

Grammerton, like other fair cities, was built on
a hill.   The highest point was the fine old Eliza-
bethan school, then and now of European reputation.   It had its proper place in the town.   Opposite to it was the old shattered and ruined castle,
overlooking the bubbling and boiling shallows of
the broad and rapid Saber.   The civil war had completed the attacks of an equally ruthless assailant,
Time—"Tempus edax rerum."   Science and war
went hand in hand in the reign of Elizabeth, and
the most accomplished scholars were the noblest
soldiers.

From this hill the town sloped rapidly down on
every side towards the river, which made it a peninsula, studded with habitations, and pregnant
with life.   Humbler as it got lower; for the great
people affected the Castle Hill, and the districts
around : and the lesser people sought the banks of
the river, where they seemed to make every use of
the water but one.

The aristocracy of the town, I say, lived on the
hills, as became it.   There was the Doctor and his

staff, learned men, fellows of universities, not
much given to horseflesh nor playing the violin,
but very useful at dinner-parties. There was the
neat little Colonel Baldhead Lethbridge, one of the
great county families, with two lovely daughters,
that we boys, for I'm an old sixth-form Grammertonian, fell desperately in love with. I've since
been informed that Clara Lethbridge was inclined
to *enbonpoint* and sallowish. At this present day I
believe her to have been a goddess; and I've an old
Gloucestershire friend who wears a wig, who will
swear the same of her sister. There was Hooper,
the great solicitor, money-lender, conveyancer of
property, agent to the old Whig families, with a
long-legged rollicking son, who was always going
out hunting, and whose whole life appeared to us
to be one of idleness and self-gratification. There
was the great physician of the county, a heavy
man in more respects than one, who turned Moore
into elegiacs as he drove about, and threw them
into his waste-paper basket, only, however, to be
picked out again and revised with care. The
second master at Armstrong's said they were not
Ovidian; but he was an old Eton and King's man,
and Dr. Bolus had been educated at Grammerton

and Oxford. Several fine old dowagers, aunts and cousins of county people, gave a tone to the society on the Hill. The lower town was composed of wharfingers, manufacturers, and the necessary adjuncts to a thriving, industrious, and very wealthy population. But money went no way in Grammerton; "blood, sir, blood, was the thing;" and so it is, to go through dirt.

These two parties were far asunder, socially and locally, only united by a few tradesmen; useful people enough, and in their innocent simplicity (for it was far removed from London) not making more than sixty per cent. of their goods. They lived metaphorically and actually on the side of the hill. The suburbs of London have reached the top. Nothing more need be said of these people, unless they fall in our way hereafter, which some of them are pretty certain to do. Yes! now I remember! The really great man of the place I was almost omitting. Jacob Handiman managed everybody, high, low, rich, poor, town and county. Beau Nash was no greater in Bath in his day, than Handiman was in Grammerton in mine.

"But who is Handiman?"

What! not know Handiman? Come, then, I'll

tell you. He's one of the most cheerful, good-natured, obliging fellows alive. Condescending to his inferiors, among whom you may certainly rank everybody in Grammerton. A great beau above all things is Jacob Handiman. His hat has a turn in it which verges on the ecclesiastical, but just cleverly escapes anything professional; his boots bear a polish which rivals all the patent leather in the world, and shows what a valet, well looked after, can do; and his feet have sufficient gout in them only to give a respectability to his walk, and restrain his energies from breaking into a run. In his case gout has been an extraordinary dispensation. His clothes were of the best and newest material, but of an earlier pattern, when trousers and coats were made to fit.

"But you haven't told us *what* Jacob Handiman was?"

Truly; it would be easier to tell you what he was not. He was a town councillor, chairman of the gas- and water-works, had been mayor so often that he seemed to be always full of beans; he was the great Conservative agent for I don't know what extent of country, or for how many counties; lessee of the Grammerton Theatre, proprietor of

the Grand Hotel; public handicapper for the district, and projector, purveyor, starter, and judge of
the Grammerton race meeting, which, under Mr.
Jacob Handiman's management, had assumed a
truly leviathan form.   To be sure, ill-natured
people said that the handicaps were made for his
friends; but his conscious rectitude was above dis-
guise, and he only laughed, as he truly observed,
the money must go somewhere, and it had better
go to his friends than his enemies.   Indeed, so
stern was his virtue in this respect, that on one
occasion he was said to have declined "to part,"
feeling that it was worse than wrong to let the
stakes go into an improper channel, or that he could
have no better friend than himself.   To do him
justice, the gentlemen all came in for their turn, if
they had but patience and horseflesh to wait long
enough for it.   In a word, there never was a better
fellow than old Jacob Handiman, or a more perfect
autocrat in Grammerton.

"Now then, Peter," said the boys, "out with
the punts; we're going to land on the opposite
side."   And a couple of punts were manned in no
time.

"Up with the flag!" said a youngster, producing

a dirty red pocket-handkerchief tied to an old stump.

"Dear heart alive," said Peter, "you're never going to——"

"You be hanged! now, Peter, none of your jaw! You've got your money, so out you go." And the punt began to move slowly in the rapidly running water, which appeared to be about four feet deep, and rushing in eddies along the narrow lanes and round the corners of the houses.

Peter himself was a great character. Peter, surname unknown, was the school boatman and bathing-man. He was hard, thin, wiry; without a hair on his face, with high cheek bones, and black twinkling eyes. At present his costume consisted of a thick striped woollen Jersey, and the biggest of blue boating trousers, well patched with divers colours about the seat, which was much worn by his boating propensities.

"Only to think; sich nice young gents," said he, soothingly. "Rebellious young wagabones (*sotto voce*), you'll spoil all your clothes. What will the Doctor say if he finds us out?"

"Never you mind; that's nothing to you, Peter."

"Now, Charon, go ahead; Mr. Tremayne's waiting, don't you see the white flag?" sung out Carloss, at the same time handing some long poles to his followers, which had been furnished for the occasion.

Thus exhorted, Peter began punting, and his subordinate followed with the second battalion, almost alongside.

Tremayne and his friends were not slow in preparing for the reception of their foes. Far from waiting to be attacked, like the Athenians at Œgospotami, on the open beach, they steered straight out to meet them. As the rival fleets met, even Peter forgot his caution, and roared in his enthusiasm, "Go it, you cripples! well done, Mr. Carloss!" as that gentleman's lance created some confusion in the leading punt of the defence. "Lud o' mercy, if we was to be cotched!"

"Keep her head straight, Peter."

"Ay, ay, sir," returned Peter, redoubling his efforts, which, from the pressure of stream, and a well-directed effort of the other flag-ship, was found to be no easy matter. The shock, however, of the boat as it struck Carloss's amidships, sent the leader and one of his followers head over heels into the water. This was, so far, satisfactory, inasmuch as it afforded undoubted evidence of the depth; and the water-babies, once on their legs, renewed the fight from the middle of the stream.

"Go it, scarlet!" shouted the crowd, which began to assemble. "Well done, white! never mind about a ducking."

"Man overboard!" said Peter. "Mind your hat, Master Simpson," as that useful article of clothing disappeared full of water.

Nothing could be more equal than the contest; for the temporary success of the attack was more than counterbalanced by a successful manœuvre of the second defending punt. She had got so well up stream, that (the young Britons, up to their waists in the water, guiding her straight towards her point) she ran full tilt into the opponents' leading boat. The punt turned over, and Carloss and his crew, Peter inclusive, tumbled into the water. When they recovered their footing, the defence was so strengthened, that it seemed necessary to beat a retreat.

"Carloss, Carloss! quick! help! Beauclerc's gone."

Carloss turned; they had neared the bridge,
where they intended to land, close by which, on
the towing-path, the stream was running with extraordinary force.   The boy had been thrown
much further than could have been expected.   As
he rose to his feet, the stream caught him and
whirled him on to the brink of the river's channel.

There was not a moment to lose.   Frank uttered
no cry; not a sound proceeded from his blanched
lips.   He turned his imploring eyes, straining with
an agony of fear, towards his schoolfellows.   His
face was pale as death, and he seemed paralysed
in all, save only when his arms were vainly
struggling with the whirl of waters.

Carloss answered the appeal; and years after
he had not forgotten it.   Seizing Peter's boat-
hook, he made his way towards his *protégé*.
As the child tottered on the edge of the deep
flood he thrust the boat-hook towards him.   Frank's
last effort caught it; and then commenced a
struggle which taxed all Reginald Carloss's strength
and weight to the utmost.   He was just able to
hold on; and Frank held on too with the tenacity
of despair.   Help was at hand.   "Dear heart
alive, if one of them young ruffians hasn't gone

and got drownded!" With which consolatory ejaculation Peter rushed to the spot, seized the boat-hook with both hands, pulled himself up to the boy, and hoisted him on his back at the very moment that Frank Beauclerc felt his limbs betraying their office. In five minutes he had had some brandy, and in ten more was running back to the schools by the shortest and quickest road his legs could carry him.

"Dinah, Dinah," whispered Carloss through the nursery door, knocking as gently as knocks can be made to be effective.

"Lor bless us and save us, what is it now?" said Dinah, not in the mildest of tempers at being disturbed from her occupation of darning stockings.

"For goodness' sake let us in and don't make a row. One of the fellows has tumbled into the water, and I want some clothes for him."

"Oh dear, dear! What will Mrs. Armstrong say? Whose things do you want?"

"Never you mind that. Give us something, and I'll give you a kiss to-morrow; only make haste. He's dying of cold."

Dinah was sixty, and squinted terribly.

"Get along with you, do; there, there's the

things, flannels and all. They're Master Gold-
dust's; he's got ever so many suits; only don't
you tell, please, Carloss. It's as much as my place
is worth."

So Frank was clothed, and became less blue by
degrees, and dried his wet things in Carloss's study;
and he vowed eternal gratitude to his friend and pre-
server; and by-and-by we shall see what came of it.

Carloss did not get a book of Homer, so Beauclerc had not to write it, which of course he would
have done; and he joined on Friday.

One week later Dr. Armstrong required some
information. "Who was the boy who had been
down to the bottom of the Low Cut, and was
nearly drowned in the flood?" So he asked the
question after evening chapel.

Six jumped up, but five sat down again. Beauclerc remained standing.

"Please, sir, it was me."

"That's bad English, boy."

"But it's true, sir, if you please."

"But it wouldn't have been less true if you had
said, 'it was I.' The verb 'to be' takes the same
case after it as before it. Did you know you were
doing wrong?"

" Yes, sir."

" What's your name?"

" Beauclerc, sir."

" Whose house are you in ?"

" Mr. Purser's, sir."

" What form ?"

" The shell, sir."

" Then, Beauclerc, of Mr. Purser's house, and of the shell, I must flog you to-morrow morning for doing what you knew to be wrong. The monitor of the shell will bring you down after first lesson.

So Frank Beauclerc was flogged, not for lying, nor for lessons, but for wilful disobedience; and Dobbs was quite right, and Mr. Colville was quite wrong. But the Doctor never forgot him, and bore him especial favour ever afterwards.

CHAPTER III.

THE COLVILLES OF LYMMERSFIELD.

Goodness resolved into necessity.—DRYDEN.

WE must go back a little way. The suburbs
of London are perhaps as beautiful as those of any
large city in Europe. They may lack the warmth
of Italy, the grandeur of Switzerland, the colour
of Eastern longitudes. As a homely, peace-loving,
picture-like variety of cultivated scenery they are
unrivalled.

Amongst the most beautiful of them is Lymmersfield. In its aspect it was uninterruptedly
rural, in its population so far metropolitan as to
exhibit comfort, not unfrequently wealth, at almost
every door. Utter poverty was unknown at Lym-

mersfield among the labouring classes; it could scarcely be called courtly, but it was eminently respectable. Everybody, that was anybody, kept a brougham.

A few years before the date of which we have been writing, there arrived in that village a clergyman, his wife, and a few children. It was the sort of family difficult to count, not difficult to name when counted, for they had their idiosyncrasies. We have nothing to do with them, particularly in this story; I mention them incidentally, because their existence exerts an influence upon their father and mother, who form connecting links with others of my *dramatis personæ*.

The Reverend Harry Colville had no preferment, incumbency, or curacy of any kind; he had given up the latter after labouring in his vocation as long and as honestly as he could. He was not impressed with the responsibilities of cold and hunger for his little ones beyond a certain point. He was rather hardworking than much-enduring; and having done what he called his best, he took four pupils and a house at Lymmersfield from an outgoing tenant.

Harry Colville had been ordained five-and-

twenty years ago. He had imbibed his notions of
discipline from a Roman Catholic lady, and of responsibility from the rector of his uncle's property.
To ride and shoot occasionally, but very well; to
play a decent rubber, and lose points and sixpences
with good temper; to carve gracefully at the
Squire's table, and not to exceed fifteen minutes
of very orthodox doctrine on Sunday.

That was theory; what was the practice?

A population of paupers; an absent squire; one
hundred per annum; typhus, dirt, smells, bad ven-
tilation; a lodging over a cheesemonger's, clothing-
clubs, Dorcas societies, daily school, Wednesday
evening lecture, tea, muffins, bad music, constant
toil, bad society, and an early marriage. The last
was the best, for it broke the spell.

The romance of a man's life is never gone, if
he be married to the woman he loves. There's a
motive for living, and a motive for living well;
and a tenfold strength of inducement is added
when there are children. They exist as a constant
antidote to trials, a constant reminiscence of God's
goodness. We seldom look at them without thinking of the Giver; and sometimes it is the only
one of his bounties which recals him to our minds

during the day. They force worldly and selfish
men to think for others as well as themselves, when
nothing else would do so. They are among the
best of Heaven's mercies. Preserve us from the
adoption of John Stuart Mill's theory on this subject, say I.

So Harry and his wife left Slavingford and came
to a comfortable house at Lymmersfield, pupils,
children, and Jock. Jock was an old pony which,
I notice, all parsons keep, however pauperised. A
Jock costs nothing.

For a woman of thirty, I think Bessie Colville
was the most beautiful person I ever saw. She sat
at the head of her husband's table making tea for
him and his pupils, who all made love to her in
their simple ways : and she shed a shower of gold
over his poverty by the brightness of her mind.
Men said she governed him, if so, it was because
she governed herself.

" Wait a moment, Harry, I want to speak to
you," said she, after breakfast, dismissing his four
pupils with an unmistakable hint.

" I'll come to you after the things are taken
away." He slipt into the greenhouse to smoke a
cheroot, and returned in the course of a quarter of

an hour. "Well, Bessie, you wanted to speak to me?"

"I did; and I do; but I dare say you are going to those boys, and I want a good half-hour. Who do you think has written to me?"

"Tom Shirley," said Harry, without a moment's hesitation. Tom was an old lover of Mrs. Colville's, and he rather expected a rise out of her.

"No, dear, not Tom Shirley; but it's an Indian letter for all that."

"I know that." And then he guessed the names of half a dozen old pupils, Civil Service, Company's Army, Queen's Service, and everything else.

Bessie said "no" to all.

"I don't know anybody else."

"Yes you do. Do you remember Everard Beauclerc, the colonel, whose property at Beauvale has been out at nurse. He stayed with us just before he went out with his young wife, eight or ten years ago."

"What, Everard? of course I do. By Jove, what a capital fellow that was; and wasn't he handsome, Bessie? We used to be great chums at Grammerton, and at Oxford, only he left without taking a degree."

" Would you like to see the letter?" said Mrs. Colville.

" Immensely; let's have it, that's a dear old soul." And the dear old soul produced a limp, but closely written, double-sheeted epistle from her pocket. She was about leaving him to its perusal.

" Oh! I say, Bessie dear, this is—that is—it's rather long; I don't think I could read the writing. You wouldn't mind reading it to me, would you?" And he proceeded to lace up his boots.

" That's very like you, Harry. You like 'immensely' to do nothing but just your own work. But here, sit down."

The letter was like an Indian letter. It contained the news of several years. Colonel Beauclerc had risen in his regiment to the command. He had shot tigers, been up the country, visited Cabul and the five rivers, been wounded at Ferozeshah, assisted at a loot, had not forgotten old England, and his dear Harry, and the old faces at Grammerton; had lost his wife, and finally had a son. All this was detailed with admirable skill; and when Bessie Colville reached this climax, she paused to take breath, and (knowing the contents to come) rather looked for some expressions of surprise. All Harry said was :

"Well, dear, so have we; several. Except the tiger hunt, it seems to be rather uninteresting for so sharp a fellow as Everard."

"Don't be impatient," said she, and resumed.

The letter went on : "My boy, who is one of the finest little fellows on earth, will leave this for England as soon as I get your answer; and pray let it be at your earliest convenience, or as soon as you and your husband can make up your minds. Will you take charge of my little Frank? He is but nine years old, very intelligent and docile; and I know nobody with whom I could place him with so much satisfaction." Then followed most liberal offers on the score of pecuniary arrangements, expressions of entire coincidence in Colville's views as to education, with only an implied wish that the boy might have the advantage of a public school, whenever the time for it might arrive.

Colville was one of those duck's backs of humanity from which troubles usually glided like water; but he had his hard trials, and the difficulty of keeping them from the woman who would willingly have borne two-thirds of them on her shoulders, added to the burthen.   It is but a mistaken kindness after all.

The letter had really been uninteresting enough to Harry Colville, and he heard but little about the campaigning of his old friend; but when she came to the proposal and the liberal conditions attached to it, he saw a pleasant addition to his income for some few years to come.   His mind, which had been looking eagerly forward to next year, when his present pupils might not be replaced, was a little upset by this very unexpected relief; and when his wife had finished reading, and looked up, she saw a very puzzled expression in his face, and a tremulous twitching of the lips, which she was at no loss to interpret, but which she thought it prudent not to notice.

"Well, Harry; that's very lucky, isn't it?   I suppose you'd like to take the boy; he'd be a companion for Charlie and Maurice."

"Take him!" said he, jumping up in the recovery of his spirits, which good fortune sometimes damped, but misfortune never, and giving his wife a kiss, which might have been heard or seen by all his household for anything he cared; "take him! I should think so. Oh, Bessie! if you only knew how anxious and wretched I have made myself thinking about next year——"

"Perhaps I do know, Harry, better than you think."

"Oh no, you don't; I take pretty good care of that." Bless the man, how clever he was in his own eyes! "But upon my word, it is so uncertain from day to day; and then one fellow thinks this ought to be taught, and another wants his son to have an occasional ride on horseback, if it is not too expensive, and a third suddenly changes his views, and requests you to send his son's books home, and the things which he left behind, and never dreams that it's customary to give or pay for a quarter's notice, that I really have lived for the last four years over a powder-magazine. However, it's all right now, Bessie, for some time to come; and you shall have a comfortable brougham, and——"

"Let's have some more furniture first in the children's room, and an under-housemaid, dear; I don't care about the brougham."

"But we can have both; and you know nobody

thinks much of one here without a brougham; only one horse, you know; I do believe it's as cheap as flys." And away went Harry Colville upon the strength of the Indian letter, forgetful of all the accidents or obstacles that might happen to rob him of his new source of income; of the thousands of miles that as yet divided him from his pupil; and of the possibility of illness or death with the boy or others, adding one more to the hundreds of disappointments he had experienced in his speculative vocation.

Mrs. Colville regarded matters from a more sober point of view; but she was not the woman to put a spoke in the wheel of her husband's happiness.

However, this time all went right. Harry's prognostications of a successful issue turned out true. There were no deaths, no quarrellings, no extraordinary demands for things which Lymmersfield could not produce, as Turkish bath, hack ponies, gymnasia, a swimming master, a professor of Sanscrit, a piano in his bedroom, or a French cook; and in the course of six months from the receipt of the letter, little Frank Beauclerc took his seat in Mrs. Colville's nursery.

"Bessie, how old is Frank?"   We have arrived at a period about six years later.

"Nearly fourteen; at least within six months of it."   Harry Colville's face lengthened, and he was deep in meditation.   He turned a few half-crowns round in his pocket; perhaps they gave him courage, for he said,

"It's time he went to Grammerton; his father and I were there long before that."   Possession brightens even a dull prospect.

"You'll be rather short of numbers the next quarter; how many go up for their examination at the end of the term?"

"Two out of the four ought to do so."

"Will they both get through, do you think?" Mrs. Colville was but a woman after all, without much ambition, and rather wished they might not.

"One of them will; and so will Temple, if they don't ask him certain questions in Euclid, or history."

"What are they like?"

"Well, his present impression is that a recti-lineal figure is contained by two lines; that Charles I. was tried and executed by William of Orange, and that Dr. Johnson was a dramatic writer in the reign of Elizabeth. That's about his form. It's no use to put those right, because he breaks out then somewhere else."

"Is Frank fit for Grammerton?"

"Yes, certainly. I'm sure his father would wish him to go; and it's better for the boy that he should."

"Well, I'm glad we didn't have the brougham, Harry; we did just as well without it."

"I can't agree with you in that. It wouldn't have cost——"

"But it would have been very disagreeable to have to give it up; and now you have the money, which you put by instead, against a rainy day."

"That's all very well; but I do think I'm beginning to be so well known now that I shall be able to command a certain number of pupils."

"Yes, dear, so you ought; for you work hard enough, and with great success; but don't forget that you've children to come after you, who want our help, as well as example."

"No, I won't: you're quite right. We'll send Frank to Grammerton, where he shall have every advantage that the school can afford him; and we must knock off the second housemaid if we

LIBRARY
UNIVERSITY OF ILLINOIS

should have a room or two empty after the next examination. And, now, if I can get out for half an hour, I should like a cigar to think over little Frank's prospects at Grammerton." He stopped a moment at the door.

"Harry," said his wife, "you look a little tired; you must go somewhere at Easter."

"That sounds very well, but her Majesty's Army Examiners have settled that question for us by fixing the examination in May. Of course no tutor can leave his pupils a fortnight before the time, especially with such peculiar notions as Temple's."

"Why don't you write to the *Times*?"

"Because it's unsatisfactory to write to any-body with the certainty of not getting an answer."

Mrs. Colville said nothing more, seeing that her husband was in a humour which scarcely wanted improving.

Frank Beauclerc went to Grammerton, as we know. His career there was more than respect-able; and we shall come back to him by-and-by. Temple escaped some of the dangerous traps to catch candidates, but not all. Having proved beyond all question that two sides of a triangle are greater than the third, he astounded his examiners by stating that fact to be "absurd." And the Reverend Henry Colville did write to the *Times*, and got no redress.

"Don't you think it would do you good to take three of the children down to Brighton, Bessie?" said Mr. Colville, when the pupils were supposed to have retired to rest. "You want to see Violet, who is gone there; and you can't have a better opportunity. You must want change."

"Nobody ought to want change who hasn't a sovereign to give for it. I want to see Violet, Harry, but Violet is well able to afford the luxury; so, suppose we ask her here when she comes back. I wish you were more prudent."

"Oh, you always say that; just as if a sovereign or two could signify. But all women are screws: more or less," added he, as he recalled a few who were not.

"Do you know what somebody says, That prudence is a necessary ingredient in all the virtues, without which they degenerate into folly and excess."

"Goldsmith says something like it, and was a

brilliant example of his own theory, my love," said
Harry Colville.

In the possession of these two people was a
store of rough diamonds between them. I think
that those which fell to the parson's share, he had
endeavoured to polish ; they looked best to the
eye ; but I am sure Bessie had much the
greater number, and they were worth the most
money.

We must go a little further back again, and
introduce some more of our puppets; after that
we shall go on more smoothly. Until we get all
the leading hounds out of cover we shall have no
chance of running into our fox.

CHAPTER IV.

MOTHERLESS CHILDREN.

The briefer life, the earlier immortality.—MILMAN.

IN a room of handsome dimensions in Southsea, facing the sea, in one of the best situations of the town, and more than comfortably furnished, were two cribs. They contained occupants of from two to three years old. The noiseless and cautious tread of a professional nurse, the anxious look of an Indian ayah who occupied a rocking-chair by the side of a low fire, the darkened windows and the heavy atmosphere proclaimed the state of the tiny occupants to be one of sickness. One was fast asleep. Its delicate little features were pale and wan. Its dark hair floated in long masses of wavy curls on the white pillow. Its breathing was heavy, and its tiny hands and limbs occasionally twitched convulsively. Still, the quiet of its long dark eyelashes gave it rather the aspect of convalescence than dangerous sickness. Not so the other : her bright colour was fixed and feverish. Her large eyes were open with an anxious, fearful gaze. She sat up in bed ; and, as her nurse tried to persuade her to lie down, the poor little girl moaned feebly. She picked with one hand the parched skin from the other, and as she tried to drink some cooling and refreshing draught, she swallowed with evident pain. Then the ayah went to her, and the child, seizing her convulsively as she bent over her, dragged her forcibly down, and began to cry. Her lips were hard and dry, and her hot breath frightened the poor woman, who burst into tears, and sobbed aloud over the sweet little face.

"There, sit down, do," said the nurse, kindly, to the Indian, leading her away at the same time, " don't 'e take on so ; you'll only make her worse."

"Oh ! oh ! my little one ! Won't she get better ?" and then the woman began rocking herself again.

"You'll only make 'em worse. Look at Miss Margaret—see how she's sleeping."

"But my little one—oh, she'll die!" And the poor child began again to toss herself about in the delirium of fever.

"We must hope for the best. Dr. Millingen says the other one's better, and the turn o' the fever 'll come to-night; so don't be down-hearted." Nurse found it very difficult to soothe a woman who understood none of her duties but such as affection prompted; and not more than half of her language. Affection is very valuable by a sick couch, but we want firmness and judgment too. In these latter the poor Indian was sadly deficient.

In a room immediately below the bedroom just described, another scene, having reference to the little sufferers above, was being enacted. Leaning forward in an attitude of anxious attention sat a very handsome woman of perhaps thirty years of age. She was more than handsome; she was very remarkable in appearance, and of a very commanding presence, in figure as well as feature. At the moment I am presenting her to my readers she was engaged in listening to an intelligent, but apparently very young man : he was explaining the nature and treatment of the disease from which the children were suffering. He was earnest; but

his voice was low in tone, as though unwilling to
disturb a reasonable sorrow, or to jar nerves strung
by manifestly painful tension. It was plain to see
suffering in the lines of the lady's face; care and
want of rest. She had done her duty, more than
her duty, of watchfulness; but a close analysis of
the expression of her face exhibited absence of ma-
ternal solicitude. The young medical practitioner
who sat opposite to her, had, however, failed to
discover this; and her manner and language
evinced a strong, if not tender, anxiety for the
safety of the invalids.

"One, then, you say, will recover. Which is
it? But there can be no doubt of that?" And
she answered her own question in a disappointed
tone, as if one were a greater personal favourite
than the other. "The one sleeping when we came
down, nearest the door. And the other, Mr. Millingen? Can nothing be done? absolutely nothing?" And she pressed her fingers to her lips,
and bit her nail with an impatience of sorrow not
common.

"It is only honest to—to—say that—well! I
won't say nothing can be done. I have tried
everything. Nature may yet do more than art.

I will return with Dr. Jones the moment he comes home: he is the safest man in Southsea. Oh! Madame Rosenfels, ours is a sad task to explain to a mother——"

"No, sir, no. You are saved that. I am not their mother. They are but cousins entrusted to my care in India: it is almost as hard a task to convey the intelligence; but not quite so bad as that. Their names are Carloss, Violet and Margaret Carloss. Poor Mary! what a blow!"

Mr. Millingen rose, somewhat relieved. He looked so very young.

"Is the nurse I have trustworthy? She was recommended by my landlady; for, as you see, I am a stranger in this place. Half Indian, half German." She spoke, however, with no accent, but remarkably well and grammatically, even for an Englishwoman; occasionally only making use of a Germanicism.

"Perfectly; and your Indian servant—— ?"

"Will do all you tell her correctly, neither more nor less."

"Then, madame, I will wish you good morning, until I can return with Dr. Jones, who may give us better hopes than I can. I think I have now

the names entered in my memoranda correctly,
Violet and Margaret Carloss? Thank you."
And Mr. Millingen took his hat and his departure
together.

When he was gone, Madame Rosenfels, as she
was called, did not go to the sick-room again immediately. She drew her chair to the fire, and sat
moodily contemplating it for some time; but she
shed no tears, and only said once or twice, " How
terribly unfortunate : poor little thing! who could
ever have thought it!" Her face reassumed its
look of impatient perplexity.

The nurse came down to report progress two
or three times. The child was just as restless as
ever: no better—her sister, as she called her, was
sleeping calmly, and was cool and comfortable.

Then Doctor Jones arrived with Mr. Millingen.
Their united ages would have been that of two
average practitioners, for the physician was an oc-
togenarian at least. Mr. Millingen mistrusted his
own youth and inexperience; he had not erred on
the same side now. I presume the two together
might have made up an average of two vigorous
intellects.

But the fact is that nothing could be done. If

all the Doctor Joneses in England, including
Wales, had assembled round that little fever-
stricken form, it was too late. That night the
baby died; and its innocent breath went up to
heaven, carrying with it the better part of life in
its death, it left a legacy of evil thoughts and deeds
behind it, like the gross refuse of some exquisite
perfume, when its essence has been allowed to
evaporate.

Dr. Jones brought no comfort to Madame when
he came down-stairs, excepting that everything
had been done which human skill could devise;
but he took away a guinea. It was a very sad
one, though given without a sigh, and well de-
served. The old gentleman had spent a life in the
patient investigation of disease in this world, and
began to reap the fruits of his labours just as he
was about to go out of it. There is no one whom
the sick man so greedily calls for as the doctor, no
one from whom he gathers such comfort, such
relief, such encouragement; there is no one so un-
willingly paid. We cannot think with Zimmer-
mann even, that the patient can oftener do without
the doctor than the doctor without the patient.
The obligation, all said and done, is not even

mutual; the patient has a great deal the best of the bargain. If he live, he has bought back what he prizes more than anything; if he die, he goes out of the world like a gentleman, with his physician by his bedside.

When the physician and the general practitioner found themselves in the street, the former very naturally offered his companion a seat in his brougham. It was readily accepted, and Mr. Millingen seated himself well forward. It served two purposes, as a modest tribute to the superiority of proprietorship, and as a letter of introduction to the promenaders on the parade.

"Who's that young fellow in old Jones's brougham?"

"His name's Milligan or Millingen, or something of that kind; seems to be in good practice. I suppose he's been to a consultation?"

"I suppose Jones does a practice of about ten thousand a year?"

"Quite that. Dunderhead gives him three hundred and fifty for a daily visit."

"Well, Dunderhead makes it pay, for he does a great deal of gambling in life insurances; and the

Doctor's information, which is drawn out of him as a mere matter of incidental conversation, is very valuable."

Whilst the passers-by speculated as largely on the messengers of death as Lord Dunderhead was supposed to do on the living, the tenants of the well-appointed brougham had their subject of conversation.

" Then my little patient cannot recover, Doctor ? "

" Nothing short of a miracle can save her; your treatment has been all that it could have been, in my opinion. But I thought it was a Mrs. Rosenfels, not Carloss ? "

" The lady is Madame Rosenfels, the child's name is Violet Carloss. She is a guardian or governess—their friends are all in India."

" A remarkably handsome woman," said the Doctor, dogmatically.

" Very," replied the general practitioner, tenderly.

" I don't know when I've seen a more striking face. Those fine dark eyes of hers, and her straight eyebrows, are singularly classical."

" They are so, Doctor Jones; and her very straight, perfectly-formed features and excessive paleness add to the effect."

" Precisely. Do you know, Millingen, I made a pretty close study of physiognomy, formerly, and I think I never saw a face exhibiting one characteristic so strongly."

" And what's that, Doctor ? "

" Can't you guess ? "

" The general character of the face seems good; and she exhibited great anxiety about the little girl; more than usual with guardians of children that belong to other people. Yet her face has no tenderness. Perhaps you mean patience ? " replied Millingen.

" You're near the mark. It's active patience, if that's not an anomaly. She has the characteristics of the most indomitable perseverance. It may be for good, or it may be for bad; of course I can't tell what her circumstances or education have been; but if she sets out on a scent she'll follow it with the tenacity of a bloodhound." The Doctor took a pinch of snuff.

" You think so ? "

" Look at her mouth, sir, look at her mouth—

real Prince's mixture." This referred to the snuff, not the mouth.

" So I did, Doctor, and it made mine water." Here the gentlemen, both young and old, indulged in a laugh. " Wonderful teeth."

" I never saw an under-jaw like that, with the same conformation of features, that did not do a great deal of mischief or a great deal of good. Let us hope it may be the latter. Here we are."

" Good afternoon, Doctor. I'm very much obliged to you." Saying which, Mr. Millingen took out his latch-key and let himself into his modest abode.

The Doctor was right. That night the baby died.

About ten o'clock the same evening the nurse came to call Madame Rosenfels.

" Is the child worse, nurse? "

" She's quieter, ma'am, but it's very near all over. Poor little thing! "

Madame Rosenfels followed her out of the room, and went up-stairs. The little thing had subsided into utter exhaustion from her previous paroxysms. Her forehead was moist, and her hair hung in damp masses round her pillow. Her eyes were half closed; and she uttered a low moan as the ayah moistened her parched and blackened lips from time to time. Madame Rosenfels came towards the bed, and looked sorrowfully on the little sufferer. She had been constantly to see them both during the few days of their illness, and the contrast was even painfully striking between her present prostration and her late delirium. She looked at her companion, who was sleeping peacefully, and in a fair way for recovery. Then she returned to the sufferer; and as she looked steadily at her, perhaps into the future, her eyes grew dim, and tears fell heavily and slowly, not in showers, over the counterpane of the little crib.

"Baba, let me have that chair." The ayah made way for her mistress, who, taking the child in her arms, and wrapping her closely in the shawls and blankets which surrounded her, pressed her closely to her bosom and sat rocking her by the fire.

The little hands played at first over the beautiful features; lisped the name of Aunty, which she had been taught; and then put its gentle heavy head upon the softest pillow that human sorrow ever knows—a woman's breast.

The breathing was loud and irregular at first. Then, as the hands grew tighter round the neck, it became calmer and more regular.

Madame continued to rock, and looked past the tiny head into the waning fire. Not a word, not a motion was heard in the room; and those large bright eyes were fixed in sad and gloomy speculation. An hour had passed, when the door-bell rang. " The doctor," said nurse; and Madame Rosenfels woke from her reverie. She listened; not to the door, or the step, as it turned into the drawing-room, but to the breathing of her little burthen. It was hushed. It was gone. How still and quiet! She put her gently down into her lap. Alas! she had gone to sleep in Aunt Ady's arms, and she never woke again.

From this period nothing remarkable happened. Time wore on. Madame Rosenfels and her little *protégée* continued to live together in the greatest comfort and harmony. The ayah had been sent back to India with a family who required her services; and Mr. Millingen had called to inquire after Madame and her surviving companion, not of course with any view to his professional services.

Madame paid his account with many expressions of gratitude for his services.

"And would you only be kind enough to correct the name of my poor little girl on your account to Margaret? Margaret Carloss, not Violet — the other is Violet. She scarcely knows her name, to be sure, as she has always been called Pet. As she gets older, we must give her her right title."

"A thousand pardons, madame, certainly. I thought our poor little patient was Violet," and then Mr. Millingen hesitated. "By the way, excuse my referring to a painful subject, but I rather think" (he might have said he was quite sure, but everybody adopts euphemisms at times) "that I gave the wrong name to the registrar at the funeral. I will see about its being corrected before it is placed upon the gravestone."

"Oh! thank you, very much, for your kindness. May I rely upon you?"

"Indeed you may, Madame Rosenfels."

Madame Rosenfels took a dislike to Southsea. Comfortable as it was, much as she valued the services of Mr. Millingen, she could not but feel the recollection of her first arrival to be painful. She should leave it shortly. What for? Two things mainly guided her. Masters for Violet as she grew up, and society for herself. Old Doctor Jones was nearly right. Madame was a woman of active resolution. In one week her bills were paid, her rooms were vacant, and she and her *protégée* were gone. Her servant, one maid to whom she entrusted her little girl, and who waited upon herself, received a month's wages, and was gone too.

Where to? That was a great question with her. A spa, a cathedral city, the seaside, or a London suburb? Leamington? Cheerful, clean, commodious, with a pretty country. Not inexpensive, though, and the sort of place where your next door neighbour knows what you have for dinner; almost whether it agrees with you or not. Bath? Just as bad, and much hotter. Cheltenham? Madame Rosenfels had no particular desire to fall into the society of old Indians. Chichester, Salisbury, Canterbury? Clerical society had no fascinations for Madame, and canons are married or unmarriageable. Brighton? She hesitated some time over this. Considered the drainage question seriously. It appeared to have most of the inconveniences of London without its conveniences. A suburb then? within easy reach of the metropolis : tolerably good society, a dry soil, a small detached house, and the sympathy of neighbours without the inconvenient intrusion of friends.

She made inquiry in town, and found on the books of a house-agent what she wanted at Lymmersfield.

" There's a small house to be let now, ma'am : you can have a card to see it. It is detached, has a small garden, and may be let for a term of years on lease, or for one. Rent moderate. Say sixty pounds a year. Stable and coach-house, small but commodious." With which, he took his pen from behind his ear, and commenced writing again, as if his life depended upon it; as the manner of such persons is."

" And the society?"

" A 1." Here he looked up, and struck by the figure before him, added, " I beg pardon, ma'am; very good indeed. We live there."

This seemed hardly to reassure Madame Rosenfels quite so much as it ought to have done. She thought, however, that it was hard to condemn the whole village for one; so she went further.

" And when could I have possession? "

" Immediately, to-day, if it suits you," said the clerk, writing away.

" Is it furnished?"

" Furnished or unfurnished are our instructions. Of course the rent is higher furnished. Eighty-five. There's a card of admission. Only half an hour from London Bridge."

" Rather a bad part of London to come to."

" Pardon, ma'am, we find it uncommon convenient." Which most likely he did, as he was writing upon Fish-street Hill.

This constant reference to " us" and " I" jarred upon Madame Rosenfels uncomfortably. Reflecting, however, that she would not probably be thrown much into the society of the young man who was addressing her, she merely added: " Then, if you will give me a card, I'll go down at once."

" Very good, ma'am," rejoined he, signing his name with a flourish. " Over the bridge, first on the left. Lymmersfield and Flummerxton Station, half an hour's drive, lovely country, sandy soil, . and beautiful church, lately built, and all open seats, quite the right thing. Morning, ma'am."

Madame Rosenfels found the house and the village nearly what she wanted. She took the

house at once; and by the time our acquaintance,
Harry Colville, arrived there, she and Violet Carloss were as much an established fact, and likely
to remain so, as the new open-seated church, the
gentlemanly grey-headed old vicar, Suet the
butcher, established in 1793, and the parish
pump. This latter institution was somewhat remarkable, for it had been erected by the kindness
of a neighbouring nobleman on some auspicious
event of his life (birth or marriage, anything but
his death, I believe), and opened by two most
worthy churchwardens and an overseer, who re-
galed the school-children from its ample resources
subsequently to their singing a hymn, com-
mencing,

As pants the 'art for cooling streams,

an obvious compliment to the professors of hy-
draulic science. The history of Madame Rosenfels,
and the relation of how she came where she was,
is too important to begin at the end of a chapter.

CHAPTER V.

MADAME ROSENFELS.

The world was sad! the garden was a wild!
And man the hermit sighed—till woman smiled.
CAMPBELL.

ADELAIDE ROSENFELS, *née* Von Gastein, had been brought up in a false position. It is the worst thing that can happen to anybody. It damps energy, misrepresents reality, encourages a spirit of petulance and discontent, and perverts valuable faculties from their proper objects to the worst exercise of their powers.

Mademoiselle von Gastein was of German parentage, but born in England. Her father had been one of those persons who, nobly born, could never have been notorious, but for one of those numerous *émeutes* which are of the utmost significance to Germans, and of none whatever to anybody else. England became his home. He might as well have been hanged in his own country for any good he was likely to do here.

He brought up his daughter with a theoretical notion of her own importance, and a practical knowledge of his own insignificance.

As she grew up she became exceedingly handsome, clever, and unscrupulous. She detected the value of an empty name in a country where there is a place for everything but incapacity. She studied perseveringly, and in process of time, in spite of father and mother, apprenticed herself in a school of some eminence; ostensibly as a sort of parlour boarder, actually as a companion and teacher of German and French; of both which languages, from the father and mother's instruction and habit of conversation, she was a perfect master. The extreme beauty of her face, as she ripened into womanhood, secured her plenty of favourites among the pupils; and as Adelaide von Gastein was intent only on making her way in life, at any cost, she attracted the elder girls by her injudicious indulgence of their foibles.

Amongst the most constant and culpable of her intimates was a weak, pretty, vain person, an orphan of good position and fortune. Mary Langley could never have been an estimable girl; but she might have been less selfish and self-indulgent, had she chosen a companion of higher principles, or one less fixed in bad ones. Interest made Adelaide von Gastein unwilling to lose sight of her; and when she left Mount Chesterton, to plunge into her vortex of London society (there are vortices enough to swallow of all sorts), her friend made a point of spending a week or two with her every three or four months, when she listened to possible marriages, and probable proposals, and exacted in return very substantial offerings for her forbearance.

When Miss Langley did really marry Major Carloss, a perfectly well-bred and singularly inane old gentleman, with an eye-glass and a wig, creaky boots, and a well-starched cravat; when she transferred herself and her Three per Cents. to the keeping of a man old enough to be her father, for no earthly reason but to avenge some fancied slight of some younger lover, Adelaide von Gastein assisted at the ceremony. A

year or two later, when the Major accepted a
lucrative post as one of the now defunct Company's servants, the two women swore eternal
friendship on the shrine of mutual convenience and
confidence; and the one gave and the other
accepted an invitation, as particular as it well
could be, to go out to India, should matters not
take a favourable turn in England.

Matters did not take a favourable turn in
England; which means that young Lord Splinter-
Bars, who had been feeling, as far as he could
feel, and expressing, but not in sufficiently explicit
language, his intense admiration for Adelaide von
Gastein, suddenly married Lady Rachel Hop-
pington, sister and co-heiress of the Marchioness
Turniptop, who made the match to save her
cousin Splinter-Bars, as she said, from a handsome adventuress. But women are very suspicious
of one another.

When Adelaide von Gastein sailed from England she was the possessor of a very small fortune;
but it was a something. Her parents had both
died; her mother some years before; her father
but lately—she was still in mourning, and it was
vastly becoming to her. From him she inherited

what remained of a property which, as he represented, had dwindled from a magnificent estate to something under a thousand pounds. If a shark is attracted by nothing short of a man's thigh-bone or a leg of mutton, a perch, when hungry, will run at anything.

Such a perch was on board the good ship *Cormorant*, bound for Madras in the autumn of 1830, in the shape of a fellow-countryman. M. Rosenfels was a good-looking man, and not so blazé by the charms of Parisian life but that he could feel for the lonely situation of so handsome a person as Fräulein von Gastein.

The voyage out was not unprofitably employed on his part. He looked like an idler; he was a gambler; who had passed through the fiery ordeals of Paris, Homburg, and Baden. Those climates did not agree with him. The homage which was due to his talents was not tendered to his reputation. He was seeking India, where he trusted to lay subaltern improvidence under contribution, and an extra thousand would be of infinite service at the commencement of his campaign. If it must be saddled with something, why not with so striking a woman as mademoiselle?

The young lady was touched. She had come out to be married; why not immediately? The strongest-minded women, and Adelaide was far from being the weakest, are vulnerable at some point. They have a tender heel, and judicious flattery points the shaft with unerring aim. On their arrival she sought the house and the counsel of her friend, who was nothing loth that her dear Adelaide should follow her own example.

It took but little time to undeceive her as to the temper, resources, and honesty of her husband. Madame Rosenfels had scarcely parted with her last hundred pounds to this worthless scoundrel (for what will not a woman do for any thing or body she loves?), when a quarrel took place at the gambling-table of some officers up the country. Monsieur was detected with the king concealed in his hand, and was kicked ignominiously down-stairs. As he had now got rid of all his money, all his credit, and the greater portion of brains he ever had possessed, he blew out the small remainder of them with a pocket-pistol. An unbeliever has just courage enough to show the world how much afraid he is of life.

No one could help sympathising with the deserted lady; and Major Carloss, who was much from home, in consequence of his appointment, was delighted to obtain for his pretty little wife so desirable a companion. Mrs. Carloss wanted nothing but some bosom into which to pour her senseless complaints of her husband, the extent of whose injustice seemed to be, that he was thirty years older than his young wife. Could any one answer the purpose better than her old bosom friend, who at the end of a couple of years' separation found herself in want of a home, and all the necessities of civilised life?

The two ladies lived very much together; for the married life of Major and Mrs. Carloss was not a happy one, and he made his visits few and far between. The Major had reason to complain, though he did not go the right way to soothe nor to subdue a frivolous, but pretty and inexperienced woman, who looked for attention and flattery as regularly as for her daily food. It would be too much at this time to say that the conduct of Mrs. Major Carloss had become criminal; it was only vicious enough to induce the suspicion that it might become so.

Circumstances favoured the conclusion.

One of the handsomest and most recherché persons in India was Colonel Beauclerc, the father of Frank, who has already been presented to the reader. A chetah hunt or two, with some wild shooting, brought him into the Madras Presidency; and as that kind of meeting seldom terminated without some sort of gambling, the least offensive form in which that fashionable vice can present itself was postponed for a "finish." The Colonel backed himself to ride one of his own chargers, which he had brought from England, against a native Arab, over four-and-twenty hurdles, distributed over three miles of country, for a considerable number of rupees. The English horse had to all intents and purposes won, when at the last hurdle, which was insecurely fastened, he slipped, and catching the top of it with his fore-legs, it came down. Unable to release his feet from the bars, the Colonel and his horse rolled helplessly over, and when the latter extricated himself the former did not. He was carried to the nearest convenient house, which happened to be that of Major Carloss, at that time the residence of his wife and her companion.

The nursing proved a long and interesting

business; and after some weeks, when the shoulder was put right, and the internal injuries were declared to be reduced, the handsome Colonel lingered in a willing captivity. He had been a widower but two years. His reputation might have been of service to his hostess if "forewarned" always meant "forearmed," but it does not; and when at length absolute necessity compelled his return to the Bengal Presidency, he carried with him no diminution of his reputation for gallantry.

It was thought that the birth of a daughter, some time afterwards, might have mended matters in the Major's bungalow. It might have been so, and frequently is. In the present case it was not. Indeed, it almost appeared that this messenger of peace was rather a cause of regret to both.

When the weak and the strong come together in mutual confidence, the weak get the worst of it. They have always something to reveal. The strong are guilty of no such infirmity, for they keep their revelations to themselves. Mary Carloss had plenty to tell, and she told it. It scarcely astonished her friend, but it is not too much to say that part of her story shocked her. Adelaide had few moral doubts about her friend's weakness, but she scarcely expected to have had them cleared up as they were. There are secrets of which it is exceedingly unpleasant to be the depository. It is but justice to her to say that she had nothing to confess, unless it were a dogged perseverance to regard the world as her oyster, and to open it. She began with her friend, and a very good speculation it was to trade on. In this partnership of infirmities she brought less capital to the concern, but had by far the more profitable situation in the firm. The senior partner sometimes sighed for more independent action, and it came to her sooner than she thought for, and differently from her expectations.

Whatever Major Carloss's short-comings as the husband of Mary Langley, he was a gentleman, and always treated his wife's guest with the courtesy due to a lady. On the present occasion he did more.

"Madame Rosenfels," said he, during one of his occasional visits, "I have a proposal to make to you, which I think may be mutually convenient; that is, if you have any idea of ever returning to England."

" I have been a long trespasser upon your kindness——"

" Not at all, madame. You have rendered me an essential service by your goodness to Mary, and I can scarcely express to you how much I feel it."

The Major was perfectly sincere, and Adelaide Rosenfels saw that he was so. She expressed her satisfaction.

" What I was going to propose to you is this. I am anxious that Violet should have the benefit of an entirely English education."

" I can easily believe it," rejoined the widow.

" I know no one so capable of superintending it as yourself."

Madame Rosenfels felt sincerely flattered.

" This little girl will have a handsome provision. I propose to settle upon her the sum of ten thousand pounds; the interest of this money to be placed in your hands to be expended in her education. I should propose to make you her sole guardian and trustee, in conjunction with an old friend of mine in England. At my death I shall leave her an additional ten thousand, should there be no reason for altering my intention in this respect."

The Major drew himself up, feeling that he was acting liberally by the little girl. Madame Rosenfels bowed a gratified smile.

"The income," continued he, "from ten thousand pounds judiciously invested, will produce about five hundred a year; and with good management I think two ladies may live upon it comfortably for the present.

Again the widow Rosenfels signified her assent to this proposition

"But I have another scheme by which the income of the lady who shall undertake this charge may be materially increased. I have a niece, of whom you have heard me speak, Margaret Carloss, the daughter of my brother Frederick: he is not rich, not so well off as he might have been; but I have thought that with the one hundred and twenty pounds a year which he proposes to add to it, a very good income may be made by taking the two children together. Now I should like your opinion of my project."

Madame Rosenfels was a lady firm of purpose; and that purpose had been a home for herself whenever she saw the opportunity of making it a desirable one.

"I think well of your project, Major Carloss. But in my position it requires consideration."

"Pray take your time, and give me an answer when it suits you to do so: there is no hurry."

"It is not so much time, as an explicit understanding of the terms. May I ask a few questions?"

"As many as you please.

"Do I understand that the control of this income will be entirely in my hands?"

"Entirely. If I had not sufficient confidence in your discretion I should never have made the proposition."

Madame Rosenfels felt more than flattered, but she knew that flattery was but light sustenance.

"The control of the property will be——?"

"In the hands of yourself and my old friend General Fletcher. It will, however, be handed over to my daughter intact upon her marriage, or upon her attaining the age of twenty-three."

It was a long time to look forward to, and a handsome income for some years.

"And of the hundred and twenty pounds a year for Margaret?"

"On precisely the same conditions. It is, how-

ever, my brother's intention to have Margaret out
again when she shall have finished her education.
Still I think that can hardly be for many years to
come."

"And the expenses of the voyage?"

"Will be defrayed by me. The money will be
properly invested in the joint names of yourself
and General Fletcher, and a year's income in ad-
vance placed to your account at your banker's, on
your arrival in England."

"May I give my answer to-morrow, Major? It
is a great responsibility, but the liberality of your
conditions holds out a great inducement."

"I am glad you think so. In the event of my
death it will be equally secure to you. Of one
thing, however, I shall warn you. Do not let
Violet indulge hopes that it will ever be increased."

"Certainly not."

"It is a great object to me, moreover, that the
cousins should be together, and that the tie should
be strengthened in every respect. My brother,
though a poor man, holds a high position, and in
every respect but that of fortune is my superior."
As the Major said this, however, he drew himself up, looked at his boots, which were of the first

order, and pushed up his neckcloth. At that moment his brother must have been a great man indeed.

Within three days the preliminaries were settled. Servants were engaged. Little Margaret and her ayah joined the Major's circle, near Madras, from the Bengal Presidency. Within two or three months adieux had been made. The ladies wept; one of them bitterly, for she was weak, the other one conventionally, for she was strong. The Major was but slightly affected; but he was the gentleman to the last, and pressed on Madame Rosenfels a very handsome present at parting. The voyage was auspicious; and thus it was that a very handsome lady and two little girls reached Southsea.

Madame Rosenfels's triumph may be summed up in a few words. A handsome income for some years, and a few confidences which were worth something whilst Mary Carloss was alive.

But life is uncertain; for one of the two children was dead within three months of her return to England. It was a contingency for which Adelaide Rosenfels had not bargained.

It was a very trying time for that lady, but she

got over it.   Two letters were despatched to India.
One plunged a father in immediate sorrow; the
other satisfied a mother that her darling was still
alive.   As to the Major, he secured a considerable
sum to the protectress of his daughter in the event
of another such calamity.

But the child grew and prospered, and learnt
very little, having but slight inclination for what
is called book-learning.   She was healthy and
wealthy, but not over-wise.   Loving and lovable
at the time we speak of, when Frank Beauclerc
was still at Grammerton, and Madame Rosenfels
occupied the detached cottage at Lymmersfield.

Major Carloss had one son by a former wife,
many years older than Violet.   He it was who
would remain in the upper fifth form at Grammerton; who would lead armies in punts; who fished
Frank Beauclerc out of the Saber with a boat-
hook; and who had joined the —— Hussars in
County Cork; good luck to him!

CHAPTER VI.

FRANK BECOMES A MAN.

Imberbis juvenis, tandem custode remoto.
Ars Poet. Hon.

Now we start fair again. Five chapters and a great deal of energy have been devoted to bringing the candidates up to the scratch. At last they are all there. About five years have transpired since our last meeting at Grammerton; and now we are coming back again to look at little Frank Beauclerc, and see what he has grown into, and what he has been doing. We can afford to leave the Colvilles and Rosenfels' elsewhere for a time till we want them. Then we can pick them up again and let them down, which makes imaginary acquaintances so much more agreeable to manage than those of real life.

Speaking of real life, by the way, I must beg of
my acquaintances not to invest themselves with the
characters scattered about in my books, nor indeed
to dress up their friends or mine in such badly
fitting robes. I can make a coat to fit, or a cap, as
well as most men; but I must protest against
this habit of regarding these pages as an old
clothes' shop, full of garments to be clapped
upon somebody or other. You see, if the waistcoat fits, the chances are that the coat does
not; or if the coat seems positively made to
order, be sure the breeches will prove baggy. If
you insist upon putting on these garments at ran-
dom, O reader, do not be disgusted or offended at
your own appearance, as a Holywell-street swell.
If you are not in such a hurry to recognise yourself
in your wretched costume, others will not be so
ready to do so either; excepting your very best
friends indeed, who have always something pleasant to say, and invariably think they have caught
sight of you, where you would prefer not to have
been found at all.

Let Strabo squint, and Pætus have a slight cast
in the eye. Strabo naturally becomes Pætus. A
knock-kneed young rascal may well style himself

Varus, and he of the club-foot become a Scaurus.
But why reverse this natural order? Why delight
in accumulating on your own head all the depra-
vity of the rascal, or the extravagance and inanity
of the fool of the story, because the one wears
the same coloured clothes or the same shaped
hat as yourself, and the other is blest with the
same superabundance of rank or resources?
What good-natured friends you must have!

But I have let slip my old acquaintance Frank,
of whose welfare I professed in the beginning of
this chapter to be curious.

What has he grown into? Legs and wings, of
course. All fellows do about the age of eighteen.
At least those do who do not become set and stiff;
and though they be strong, they have not those
characteristics of elegance and activity which are
essential in heroes, from the fashionable highway-
man upwards. He had good honest open eyes,
which looked men straight in the face—and women
too, sometimes, very much to their detriment. It
was a fine manly face, with a certain amount of
softness about it, which did not belie the natural
character, but which was all the better for the
capital training it had undergone.

And what has he been doing? Not a great
deal, I admit. His intellect was made for wear,
not for show. "It would wash," so I think Swan
and Edgar would have described it. *Fast* colours
in the human subject do not always wash; only
occasionally. What has he been doing? His pro-
nunciation of French was execrable; but, having
professed to learn it, he was not ignorant of that
language. Arithmetic he believed to be useful in
his intended profession, and mathematics generally,
but he did not know much of either yet; he could
construe extempore a moderately difficult passage
of a Greek and Latin author or two, enjoyed
Thucydides and Herodotus, appreciated the wit of
a language more than its construction, and wrote
good Latin verses. Knew a great deal of Grecian
history, but was not so fond of the Romans, whom
he regarded as of a harder nature than the Greeks.
Was no great hand at the "ologies," and always
averred that the first step to success was the study
of the things that lived on the crust of the globe,
and afterwards those that were buried inside it.
In fact, his friends called him a very sharp fellow,
which he was not; but he had been doing enough

to become a good scholar, and to have balanced his mind in such a manner that difficulties were sure to vanish before his application.

His last day at Grammerton has arrived. It was the last day of the summer half, the examinations were over, and to-morrow Frank Beauclerc would be a man. So he thought or tried to think. We have many of us had our last days, and felt very much in the same manner. Few of us so modestly. But we have managed to pull through, all of us, with something to be thankful for to our school days, and so will he.

It is a good warm summer's afternoon, time ten minutes to seven, when the stumps are to be drawn, and the match too, unless one side or the other can manage to win in that time.

The gentlemen of Grammerton and the county are playing their annual match with the school; and there are plenty there to whom it is the great occasion of the year. They are playing in the school close; and the walk round it and the marquees are full of company. The ladies have not on their worst bonnets, bibs, and tuckers, for the occasion, you may be sure.

There are twelve runs to get, and ten minutes
to do it in; and the last of the school eleven is
just going in, the ninth wicket having fallen.

"I say, Beauclerc, why haven't you been in
before?"

"Because the captain desired me to go in last."
Saying which he finished the last buckle of his
pad, and began walking towards the wicket as he
drew on his glove.

"What a shame of Scorewell not to have put
him in before; don't you think so, Tremayne?"

"What a young ass you are," says Tremayne;
"just as if Scorewell doesn't know his own
business best."

"I know why he puts him in last," joins in
young Culpepper. "He wanted a steady man at
the end, to keep his wicket up, while somebody
else got the runs. And you see it's all right.
There's Slogger's got his eye in for hitting, and if
we've luck we shall just win."

"By Jove! there goes old Goldicott, with his
cheroot: they're going to put on the slows.
That's to play against time. What a shame!"

Old Goldicott, of the Priory, Grammerton, was
an old Grammertonian, and an immense favourite

with the boys, except when he played against them. He had been long time a dweller in Hindostan, and had returned to live in his own and father's and grandfather's native place, with an ample, if not a very large, fortune. Nothing went on in Grammerton well without him, from a cattle-show to a new pump; but he was never so happy as when he was playing football or cricket with the boys, or indulging some of them in any legitimate way he could think of.

"Well bowled!" shouted the elders, as they saw one of Goldicott's slows drive Frank Beauclerc nearly on to his wicket.

"Well played!" shouted the youngsters in return, as they saw it placed safely to mid-wicket off. The field came a little in, as it seemed clear that Beauclerc's was not to be a hitting game.

The next ball was not quite so good, and was put away between short-leg and the bowler for one run.

Nobody spoke now, for the matter had become serious. The field almost imperceptibly widened itself. Goldicott, too, felt a little nervous, for Slogger was in fine hitting form, and not likely to let off a loose one.

It was, however, anything but a loose one; and
even Ashford, the reverend gentleman who kept
wicket, and was an old Gentlemen-and-Players
man, could not help an exclamation as he took the
ball within three inches of the top of the wicket,
and returned it to the bowler.

"Another coat of paint wanted !" shouted the
young scoundrels from the tent—and then came
the last ball of the over. It was pitched a trifle
too far, and Slogger hit it for four. Yells from
the Lilliputians, who, however, were reminded of
their bad manners by the fifth and sixth forms,
and some not complimentary allusions to the Eton
and Harrow matches of last year.

Seven to win, and two more overs to do it in.

Oh! for youth, and hope, and the opening
scenes of the drama once more ! Should we spend
it in knocking about a ball with a block as senseless as ourselves; in stirring up the blood with
such unprofitable enterprise, instead of oiling the
mind from the midnight lamp, and wrestling to
the death with the realities of life? Indeed we
would, and we would knock it twice as hard, and
twice as often, were that, forsooth, possible, which
in our own case it is not.

Play: "Who's bowling at this end?" inquired Culpepper, of the fifth.

"Don't you know? It's Lord Legbail's brother —he's a swell, he is."

"But can he bowl?"

"Can't he just! that's all!" says Tremayne, whose English was about fit for the remove, I presume. "Such a pace, too!"

"That will suit Beauclerc; he can hit fast bowling," replied the other.

The truth of the remark was verified by a sharp clean cut into the hands of point, who, however, let it drop, and the youngsters, being quick between wickets, stole one run.

"Rather a hot one," said Mr. Funckham's friends.

"Well fielded," shouted his enemies; for which a fourth-form boy got a licking from Culpepper. I remember at Grammerton we rather prided ourselves on our good manners; they were best, however, when we were in company.

The next ball was a rattler; but one was scored for a "bye."

"That comes of wearing pads to stop in," said the miserable sinner who missed it.

" What's the score ?" said the players.

" Five to win," said the scorers.

"Play it out," shouted the youngsters. The morning of life is the time to play out every-thing.

Beauclerc stood well at his wicket. He had a good eye, and played with great steadiness. There was time to win, but it wanted a hit or two to do it. The ball came fast, well up to the bat, but was wide of the wicket to the leg; it was just the ball to be hit by a free hitter, but required decision.

"A tenter," shouted the young ones again: "three for the tent," said they, as the ball fell within the ropes, and rolled behind the canvas. Only two more; their ardour was irrepressible. To have stopped them now would have been as impossible as to have pulled up a "rusher" in front of a double post and rails when he has been once set going.

The over finished with no more. Two to win; and Goldicott lit another cheroot after a short consultation.

"Those beastly slows," said Beauclerc to him-self, as Goldicott took a gentle hop on one leg, a peculiar run of very short steps, and delivered a ball which looked slower than ever. The field closed in round the bat, but there were no effects.

"Well kept down."

The next ball was equally good, and equally well played. Two more runs to get and two more balls. The Doctor was out, and his wife was out. The more lovely daughters of a lovely mother were there; and one of them felt a— shall we say sentiment?—for this fortunate youth, Beauclerc, which only wanted careful encouragement to have developed into *la belle passion*. They would have lost the match had he known it. As it was, he saw them, and regarding them as mortals, played accordingly.

The ball was bowled by no means so straight as its predecessors, and Frank, taking advantage of the opportunity, cut it clean past cover-point with such hearty good-will that the runs were called before the ball was stopped.

He was chaired on the shoulders of a couple of unlettered giants, pressed for that purpose, and received with a cordiality that would have damaged a less enduring back than his. It was a fine finish to his career at Grammerton.

"Where are you going?" said a hundred voices. "Where are you going, Beauclerc? Come into my study; there's tea all ready." "Tarts and rum punch," said another, clandestinely, "in number six."

"I hope you are not engaged, Beauclerc," said the Doctor.

"Indeed I am. I am so sorry, sir, but——"

"Not a word, my good fellow, not a word. We wanted to take leave of you once more; but you're going to sup with my old friend Goldicott. It's better for you; you'll leave with a happier impression——"

"No; really, sir." And Frank began protesting, with great truth; for he loved the Doctor, though he preferred supping with Goldicott.

"I knew you had leave to go. I ought to have recollected it; but come and say good-bye to us to-morrow before you go for good. Come to luncheon." And the fine old scholar-like gentleman walked slowly away, followed by the young ladies and the three best boys in the school to partake of his hospitality, but whom he did not like half so much as the gallant fellow who had just won the match for them.

Tom Goldicott was better known than any man within a circle of ten miles of Grammerton. His father had lived there before him; but that is not the only reason for his popularity. He himself left the Priory, which was but a better sort of villa, when he had passed at Haileybury for the Company's service; for he did not think that a man who hunted on two horses was justified in making an eldest son an idler. Ten horses would have been different, he said. Then he would have shared the honour and the profit, and been thankful. As it was, the patrimony was not enough to do good with after his enlarged views, and was sufficiently tempting to lead him into evil. "No, no! my brothers and sisters will want their share; and as I should like to come back and live in the old house like a gentleman, without robbing them, I'll go to India. Warren Hastings can't have stripped all the Begums bare on that immeasurable peninsula: besides, some more must have grown up since then. I'll go and see what I can do."

So he went away, and he never came back again until his father's death; and then brought rupees enough to enlarge the house, and clean out the ponds, and take care of his sisters, and subscribe

to the charities, and farm high, and breed short-
horns and long fleeces, and to take an active leading part in every association that was likely to do
good to his country. By the Grammerton fellows
he was idolised. They ran their paper chases over
his farms, went birds'-nesting in his hedgerows,
fished his water, jumped his gates, and established
a right of way for themselves over his enclosures;
and in return for it all, they shouted his name on the
speech-day after the Queen and the Royal Family,
and received it with equally vociferous applause. In
fact, he had come back at five-and-forty as much
a Grammerton schoolboy as he had gone out at
eighteen; and no cricket-match between the town
and the county, or the school and the old Gram-
mertonians, would have been considered perfect
without Tom Goldicott. They would have preferred him to George Parr. He presided at the
dinners, was chairman of the board of guardians,
a justice of the peace, great at open-air festivities,
archery parties, and pic-nics; and when a happy
accident made an opening in the county, you may
be sure that Tom Goldicott proposed or seconded
somebody on the Conservative interest. He always
gave the bishop a dinner when he came to confirm

the people, in pity to the excellant diocesan, who preferred the Priory claret and delicate fare to the Rectory port and the roast and boiled of the unambitious vicar.

And this is the man towards whose house, as a wind-up of the summer half, Frank Beauclerc and eleven of his companions are making their way to supper. We call it supper because it took place at nine o'clock; a sociable meal after a cricket-match, which released us from some of the formidable courtesy of a set dinner; and pleasanter, when we take into consideration the time of year.

" Beau, you are a great swell, it seems to me. You know that the eldest girl is engaged to young Peckwater; they're to be married as soon as he takes his degree. So that's no go."

" I can't return the compliment, Slogger, old fellow; you look as if you hadn't seen soap and water for a fortnight. And that coat of yours——"

" Ah! I know. Well, I couldn't help that, you know; 'cos that Dinah had gone and packed up all my things to go to-morrow."

Dinah at Grammerton was something like majesty; Dinah never died.

" That's a pity; because the youngest girl isn't

engaged to be married, and you don't know what a clean shirt does for a fellow who isn't accustomed to indulge in the luxury often."

" Oh! come, hang it; that's too bad, Master Beau. It is clean; for I took it off Lather's bed, as I couldn't get at one of my own."

" That's good," said Beauclerc, laughing, in which the rest joined, as they turned into the Priory gate; "that's rather good. It's the one Lather has just taken off. But he's not a fellow that ever exerts himself much, so I dare say it will do."

Whatever qualms might have been felt on the score of dress-coats or patent-leather boots, they were set aside at once by the appearance of Tom Goldicott himself at the door to receive his guests, in a beautifully clean suit of white jean, and smoking a Manilla cheroot. He was a scrupulously neat person, but had imbibed his notions of propriety in a school of his own. The boys were at their ease at once.

There was a Mrs. Goldicott—a small, bright-eyed, pretty woman of forty, who had been married young, She was Indian all over—her dark eyes, inenergetic manners, and luxurious shawl; it was a favourite article of toilet with her.

"My dear, I think you know most of these gentlemen? Frank Beauclerc's father is an old friend of yours in India."

Mrs. Goldicott shook hands with them all, as they came up in a shy manner, in Indian file (out of compliment to their host, as Frank told them afterwards), and then made room for Beauclerc on the sofa.

"Your father; oh! was that your father that we knew at Calcutta? The most charming person I ever knew. You're very like him, only rather younger-looking."

Beauclerc laughed. "Well, I suppose I ought to be; as he's my father, he's sure to be the elder of the two."

"Of course," said the little woman, falling back on a cushion; "but it's twenty years ago I'm thinking of; so, you know, it wasn't such a stupid speech after all."

"Stupid——?" and Frank began to stammer apologies, when Tom Goldicott came to the rescue.

"I've seen your governor (the best of fellows

are often a little unrefined in their language)
several years later than Mrs. Goldicott, who came
home long before me.   He's the youngest and one
of the most agreeable men in India."

"I remember him well.   He was very young-
looking twelve years ago."

"Why, how old were you when you first came
to England?"

"About eight, I think."

"Would you know him if you met him to-
morrow, Beau?" said one of the small Grammer-
tonians, in a confidential tone, to his senior.

"I don't think I should, quite, unless I expected
to see him."

"I say, what a rum thing it must be not to
know your own governor."

"Surely not for you, Dufferling, because it's a
wise child that knows its own father."   And then
Tom Goldicott, having administered his witticism,
turned attention away, with a good-natured laugh,
from the discomfited one, by introducing Slogger
as the hero of the day.

"Mrs. Goldicott, you'll be delighted to make the
acquaintance of Slogger, who distinguished himself

exceedingly against us; in fact, Slogger won the match."

It will be perceived that Tom Goldicott was a bit of a *farceur*, and felt bound to keep his guests amused till the supper was on table.

"No, sir," said a matter-of-fact youngster; "it wasn't Slogger; it was Beauclerc won the match with that beautiful cut to cover-point."

"Well, then, come along, young 'un, and we'll drink both their healths."

So Mrs. Goldicott led the way with Frank, while Slogger followed with Miss Goldicott, a very pretty girl in a maze of white muslin and cherry-coloured ribbons, and Dufferling closed the procession with a second edition of the muslin and ribbons, only, being bright-haired, in blue. A miscellaneous rabble (Tom Goldicott *magná comitante catervâ*) hung upon the steps of the advanced guard.

Nothing could be better than the supper, excepting the appetites.

"Well done, Slogger!" said the jolly old Indian, from the top of the table. "How do you feel now?" Slogger had just passed on the claret-cup to Tremayne. "How do you feel now?"

" Awfully jolly!" said the Slogger, recommencing on the viands.

" I'm glad to see old Armstrong doesn't neglect your English."

" I don't understand exactly, sir," replied he.

" I mean, that some young gentlemen and ladies of my acquaintance find everything ' *awful jolly,*' which is not such good grammar as yours, that's all." Here he looked at his youngest daughter, who said, " Oh! pa," and pressed her handkerchief to her face with a becoming modesty. " Now, boys, let's drink Dr. Armstrong's health. If it hadn't been for him, you youngsters wouldn't have been here to-night, for I meant to have had the eleven. Have some more tart, Chesterton ? "

" Not any more, thank you," said the boy, who was a most jovial-looking little fellow, and whose appearance belied his abstemiousness.

" I think Chessy could do it, Mr. Goldicott, if he might stand up to it," suggested his neighbour, who had made great play with the champagne and claret-cup, whatever abstinence he had observed among the tarts and custards.

" Thank you, my dears. Now my fan; thanks; and now my gloves; they are somewhere under-

neath the table." Upon which there ensued a
dive of little heads, which returned with the scattered treasures among them; and then Mrs. Goldicott prepared to go. Frank Beauclerc, Slogger,
Tremayne, and one or two of the oldest of the
party, who did not appreciate such an address, but
left that part to the lower schoolboys, rose at
once, and bowed that lady out with a vast amount
of full-grown courtesy. The young ladies followed. The boys lost nothing of their claims in
their hands: they were regarded and treated with
considerable hauteur after their social meal. Both
parties played at ladies and gentlemen to perfection. Slogger never felt the least uncomfortable
in his second day's linen and week-day clothes
until he was addressed with such profound polite-
ness by Miss Isabella Goldicott; then for the first
time he regretted Dinah's obstinacy or precipi-
tancy, and his own want of a dress-coat. It is a
comfort to think that it had not affected his
appetite. His sense of dignity came too late for
that.

"Now, young fellows, I'm not going to get you
into a row by keeping you here too late. I promised the Doctor you should be home by eleven.

You've half an hour more, so make the most of it."

Then the conversation became general; that is, it varied from cricket to football; from jolly fellows to beasts and sneaks. A corner was kept for our big brothers, and somebody's pony took a prominent part in it. There was a mention of a pic-nic *at our place*, and a young cockney was great on theatres. Frank Beauclerc has found a ready informant on Indian life, and an interesting theme in the scrapes, talent, good looks, and popularity of his own father. Slogger and Tremayne were arguing the merits of the last University boat-race, the former maintaining that the boat was in fault, and that the stroke had injured his wrist the day before, the latter offering to lay the most frightful odds on Oxford for next year, and pulling out a small memorandum-book and gold pencil-case in earnest of his intentions.

Presently it was time to take leave; so the well-fed and judiciously-liquored little rascals pressed around Mrs. Goldicott, and offered her the choice of some very warm hands. She shook one or two, but the exertion was too much, so she sunk back and nodded a general "good night," distinguishing Slogger by name. The young ladies bowed with much graceful condescension.

"I hope when your father comes home, he will come to see me, Beauclerc," said Mrs. Goldicott, tendering him a hand, "and that you will come with him. We shall all be very glad to see you again, shan't we, girls?"

"Oh yes, mamma!" said both of them at once, presenting the object of their newly-aroused inclinations with a hand as they spoke.

"Beauclerc, I'll walk with you a little way. I shan't be long, my dear." And lighting a cheroot from a taper on the mantelpiece, he opened the door and followed Frank.

"What a handsome boy," said the mother; "so like his father."

"Charming young man," said the girls. "Did you see his studs, mamma?"

"And Mr. Tremayne says he's very clever; he's going to leave to-morrow to go into the army."

"He'll have a very good fortune, too, girls. His father has, or will have, the Beauclerc pro-

perty, besides a good share of the Anglo-Banian
Bank."

Isabella looked down at her blue ribbons and
white gauze, and Miss Goldicott smoothed down
her hair, which was certainly magnificent, and
naturally *crépu*.

Frank and his late entertainer turned through
the garden gate towards the town of Grammerton.

"Will you have a cheroot, Beauclerc? I don't
often offer one to you fellows, but I suppose the
last night of the half there's not much harm;" and
he held out a small cigar-case.

"No, thanks! The fact is, I was caught, and I
promised Armstrong not to smoke again while I
was here. I don't think I'm exempt till to-morrow
morning."

"You're quite right, having made the promise,
to keep it to its legitimate end; besides, it's a very
bad habit for young fellows to get into."

"I shall begin to-morrow."

"You don't really like it?"

"Do you, Mr. Goldicott?"

"Well, as a matter of habit; once I did it out
of opposition."

"Just so. Perhaps I do so too. But I remember years ago vowing that I'd smoke when I was my own master, because I saw Mr. Colville do it, and he looked so comfortable in the middle of all his troubles."

"Who is Mr. Colville?"

"He's a private tutor, at whose house I've lived since I came to England, and to whom I'm going to-morrow."

"A private tutor! poor man! then he must have wanted a narcotic. I wonder whether he is a relation or connexion of a family of the name of Carloss?"

"Yes; a distant one. There's a little girl, at least she's about fifteen, lives in our village, named Violet Carloss."

"Violet Carloss! Then he's the same man I recollect years ago; he was a fellow of Trinity."

"And a very good fellow too, I can tell you; and such a nice woman his wife is. I'd just as soon be with them as at my own home. Besides, I expect my father home in a year or two."

"And do you know the Carlosses, too?" Old Goldicott seemed to be still absorbed in his own reminiscences.

"You forget. I have never been in India since I was quite young."

"True; but your father was very intimate with them. The women were very good-looking; and all the good-looking women liked him. He was a great favourite of Mrs. Goldicott, I can tell you. There was a very handsome German woman, too, a sort of companion, who lived with them, a Madame —— What's-her-name."

"Rosenfels, perhaps," suggested Frank, who seemed to have nothing better to say.

"Rosenfels, to be sure it was; how the deuce did you know that? The women seem to have made some impression upon you, though you have forgotten the old Major. Ah! he was a gentleman, though rather of the slow school. He was a good officer, too, and as brave as a lion. He only died three years ago. But what makes you recollect Madame Rosenfels so well?"

"She lives in Lymmersfield. So of course I know her. But I recollect nothing about her. I believe the Carlosses were in Madras when we were in Calcutta."

"Ah! not your father, Beauclerc, for I've seen him up at Carloss's, in the hills, after a fall, or an accident of some kind." After smoking a few minutes in silence, Goldicott said, "Violet Carloss with Madame Rosenfels; oh! I see now. I suppose Violet is the Major's daughter, and came home with her."

"Yes; Major Carloss was her father. I know this only from the Colvilles, for I have scarcely seen her half a dozen times in the last five years; and I didn't know her at all before that. Madame Rosenfels must have been very handsome indeed. I've seen her in church; and she has been at the Colvilles', but not when I was there."

"Be careful, Beauclerc; she's said to be a very clever woman; and Miss Violet ought to have a little money. There was something not quite right between the Major and her mother, I quite forget what; some sort of unpleasantness. However, they are both dead now, and I suppose the girl will have her mother's fortune. Her half-brother was here a few years ago."

The old Indian had finished his cheroot; they stood before the school-house, and it was eleven o'clock. He shook hands with Frank Beauclerc; begged his regards to his father when he wrote, and wished him success in the course of life he had chosen. One went to bed to think of the career that was opening before him, to sleep upon the roses that appeared to strew his path with sweets from the morrow's dawn; the other to remind his wife of their former cheerful friend and companion, Everard Beauclerc, and to ask her whether she recollected the Carlosses and other people, and, above all, a very beautiful Madame Rosenfels, in the Madras Presidency.

Mrs. Goldicott would fain have gone to sleep, thinking that bed was made for that, and life for bed; but her husband roused her by a rather pertinent question or two.

"Madame Rosenfels? of course I do," said the lady, rather tartly, seeing that Mr. Goldicott among others had been slightly smitten by the charms of the humble companion and adventuress.

"And don't you remember that pretty little

Mrs. Carloss? There was some sort of row between the Major and his wife; not exactly a separation; but something, I've forgotten what. I thought Frank Beauclerc might have heard of it, being much with Indian people.

"Why, Tom, you don't mean to say you have been asking that handsome boy about the Carlosses and their business?" and the lady raised herself in bed.

"Indeed I do; why shouldn't I? There's nothing wrong in it, I suppose?"

"There, go to sleep, you stupid old man. Why, it was that boy's father, Everard Beauclerc, that was supposed to be the cause of the quarrel. It's well it's no worse. I forgot all about it. However, it's clear the boy has never heard of the scandal. So good night."

A quarter of an hour later our old friend Tom Goldicott was fast asleep, and regardless of all intrigues, Indian or British; while Mrs. Goldicott, in spite of her soporific nature, woke up occasionally with a languid laugh at her husband's blunder, and a malicious regret that he hadn't made the remark to the father instead of the

son.   The little woman remembered that it took a
little time to forgive the Colonel on his return to
Calcutta, and that nothing but the habit of deal-
ing with the Beauclerc peccadilloes leniently got
him into favour again.   So true it is that one man
may steal a horse, when another must not be seen
looking through the stable window.

CHAPTER VII.

A REAL WOMAN.

ὦ καλλιφεγγὲς ἡλίου σέλας.—EUR. *Troiades.*

"HARRY, you look tired," said Mrs. Colville. For we must change the scene from Grammerton to Lymmersfield.

"I look as I am, my dear; and these Army Examiners have done me out of part of my vacation again. You know I got no Easter, because they had fixed the examination for May : and now I must go on till August." It was a warm day in June, and Harry Colville gaped at the anticipation.

" Who are going up this time? "

" Standish : he's sure to come back again. He's been educated entirely on the modern system, and consequently knows nothing of English. Bentley has been taught nothing in the world but Latin and Greek : so that he's pretty sure to be plucked for Mathematics and History. Still he may pull through, for it has taught him to spell his own language, and to write the essay of a scholar and a gentleman ; thanks to his classics."

"And Frank? What do you think of him? He comes to-morrow."

"I should think Frank is quite safe, thanks to your teaching when he was a child, and Dr. Armstrong's since he has been a schoolboy. Ah! it's an ill wind that blows nobody any good. If he likes to go on reading at once, I can get him through in August ; and then I shall not regret the labour."

" Harry, you never regret labour for other people."

" I never regret it for you and the children, my

love ; and some day or other we shall be repaid for it—at least I always think so."

"One thing you're not deficient in."

"What's that?" And her husband looked up a little faintly.

"Courage. You've had enough to try yours. If you were not a good man, you would have ceased to believe in any one."

"I don't believe in many men, Bessie; but I have never ceased to believe in God."

Bessie Colville stooped down and kissed his forehead. "Yes; He's been very good to us sometimes when we least expected it. We'll continue to trust in Him. I have but one sorrow."

"What's that, my wife?" And Harry got up and looked at her with a hand on each shoulder. He thought for the ten thousandth time that he had never seen so beautiful a face. And so it was. It was just the face to give expression to every word that she uttered, as she slowly replied, "I never can help you;" and then he saw her eyes fill with tears.

"You never can help me? That's very unfortunate indeed, Bessie. You are a great incum-
brance. You know neither Greek, Latin, nor
mathematics. The Binomical Theorem would be
a sad puzzle for you. And yet I prefer you, as
you are, to a profound graduate, an LL.D. and an
A.S.S.; and without such a helpmate I think I
should have died. So don't fret, dear; and then
I'll give myself a holiday, and we'll go out for a
stroll. Where are you going to put Frank Beauclerc?"

"Into the spare room."

"It's a bore to give that up."

"Not at all. It's a blessing, Harry, to think
that we're obliged to do so."

"Let him have my dressing-room."

"Certainly not. We can do without company
for the present, at all events; and when the house
is clear of your natural enemies we shall have room
for everybody. What an odd person Madame
Rosenfels is, Harry!"

"Mysterious looking. But very pleasant and

handsome. Next to you, the best-looking woman in this neighbourhood."

"Beauty is a man's weakness: the thickest of coverings for the concealment of defects; you never see beyond it, and seldom try to do so."

"It's a letter of recommendation, dear, which one is bound to read. But what has Madame been doing?"

"Since Major Carloss's death gave us some sort of interest in Violet, she has seemed more than ever desirous of keeping the girl to herself. She is of an age now to see some society; and though I have avoided any great intimacy hitherto, I think it is our duty to do something for her."

"Now Frank's coming home, certainly." Colville suspected a woman's weakness.

"Nonsense. Frank's nothing to her, nor she to Frank. Besides, he'll soon be in a cavalry regiment, with other companions, and forget Lymmersfield altogether."

"Not if I know him, Bessie. He'll never forget you. There goes Madame."

As he spoke, a very handsome, well-dressed woman walked slowly by the front of the house. She was tall, above the middle height, and walked with a firm, well-assured step; her veil was down, light with dark spots on it, giving a delicate appearance to her complexion. She half halted at the gate of Colville's house, as though hesitating to go in; but continued her course again unchanged.

"How well she wears," said the mistress, looking at her figure.

"What a complexion!" thought the master, re-collecting the veil, and what he had seen through it. "If all veils were like that there would be more women ready to take them."

In due time of course, as in due course of time, Frank Beauclerc arrived safely at Lymmersfield. I say of course, for had an accident happened to him this story would have come to an untimely end: besides, he did not travel by the Eastern Counties. He lost his luggage naturally, and got it again at the end of four days: that came of finding himself on the South Western.

When he did reach Lymmersfield he was heartily welcomed by Colville and his wife: for it was impossible to have lived or been in any close connexion with Frank Beauclerc without liking him. Standish lent him shirts, and Bentley found him a sufficiency of external toilette for dinner, until the superintendent of the lost luggage-office and the telegraphic wires enabled him to ascertain that his chattels had gone on to Sommerfield, on the other side of London. The two words ended in "field," which was considered a valid excuse by the railway officials, and reluctantly acquiesced in by Frank.

He had not been very long back at his old tutor's, when a novel impression was accidentally made upon him. It ought to be premised that Frank Beauclerc was not a susceptible person. He was as little so as anybody. Like other schoolboys, he had experienced *soupçons* of the tender passion of course. One was very early in life: he was about ten, and the young lady eighteen. He showed her every attention by gathering for her quantities of gooseberries and currants (it took place in the warm weather), by sitting near her at all meals, and by weeping copiously when he left her. To be sure he was going away from a garden full of fruit, and a pond with a punt in it, to the elements of Latin poetry and the verbs in $\mu\iota$, which might have had something to do with his tears. However, let us be generous: he was touched.

I do not count the young female who dealt out the cheesecakes to the boys at Grammerton. For a pastrycook she was very pretty: and there can be no doubt that Frank had preferred the cheesecakes dealt out to, him by hand. Many went further than this, of course; but it was the extent of Frank Beauclerc's passion, so long as he liked cheesecakes, which was not beyond the forth form or the shell. Tom Skelter was devoted, and he was a big fellow. He wrote a beautiful copy of Latin verses to her, headed "Ad Cloen," beginning:

Te quando aspiciam, curæ solvuntur amaræ
Insolitos risus reddit imago tua,

with some more lines equally original. One indeed was so original as to have in it a bad false quantity, which was detected by Dandy Calthorpe, to whom Fanny Tarts showed them, asking for a construe. It covered poor Tom Skelter with confusion to think that his inamorata did not understand Latin, and saved him from much future trouble. Dandy Calthorpe, who was a great fool in everything but Latin verses, came back from Oxford and married Fanny. His family, very judiciously, refused to do anything for him in this country, and sent him off to assist in raising the population and reputation of our colonies, whence he has not yet returned.

Of all these things, and such hallucinations, Frank was guiltless. He had dearly loved Mrs. Colville, and the good-humoured woman who tucked him up and sung him to sleep when a little boy. Beyond this he was heart-whole.

One morning, while Mrs. Colville was superintending her garden, and while Frank was reading by the window which opened on to the lawn, the door opened, and a young girl of extraordinary beauty stood before him. As soon as she saw that

the room was untenanted except by himself, she
turned abruptly round, saying, "I beg your pardon,
I was looking for Mrs. Colville."

Frank Beauclerc was rather taken aback by the
vision, which came between him and his "remarkable events in the lives of the kings of the House
of Tudor." Although the face was altered since he
had last seen it, which indeed had not been for two
years or more, there remained sufficient resem-
blance for identification, so he called out:

"Why, Miss Carloss, is that you? Mrs. Colville
is here; through the window."

Violet turned round, and saw not Mr. Bentley,
nor Mr. Standish, nor any other of the numerous
pupils which filled up Colville's house even to the
spare room, but the face of a person whom she had
not seen often, but of whom she felt that she must
have a sort of instinctive or necessary knowledge.
She had some difficulty in recognising him at first;
then the old boyish chubby face came out in the more
oval shape and manly look which he had acquired.
The neat, trim, tight figure of the lad, however,

was gone with his round jacket, and there was
nothing of it left in the lengthy, active, loosely-set
limbs and broad pliant shoulders, which rose from
the chair to the height of a good six feet.   When
she saw who it was she laughed, however.

"And why did you call me Miss Carloss, if you
knew me?"   And they shook hands.

"What was I to call you?" said Frank, somewhat amazed.

"Violet, to be sure; what do you think?"

"Does everybody, that knows you, call you by
your Christian name?"

"Of course they do," said the lady, looking
equally surprised.

"What, Standish, and all the fellows here?"

"No, they don't know me; at least, not in that
way."

"In what way?"

"Why, not as you do—not when we were children together."

"That's true, Violet," said Frank, musing ; "it
makes a great difference."

VOL. I.   K

"Besides, we both came from India," added the girl, who looked as English as a girl well could look.

"That's something more: so our interests are partly identical."

"I don't know what you mean, Frank, by our interests being partly identical; but when I've known people a long time, and we've played together when we were children, I don't like them to call me Miss Carloss; and now we'll go to Mrs. Colville, if you'll tell me where she is."

When Frank began to consider the simple rationale of the young lady's request, he was not inclined to judge her very harshly. He reflected that she was scarcely seventeen years old, and was not likely to calculate results; so he accepted his position with a good grace. Besides, it was a very lovely face, and not of a character to make any one sceptical as to its unaffected simplicity. Mrs. Colville was deep in the mysteries of a ribbon-border, which was to rival all the ribbon-borders in the county for colour, though it was likely to yield to that of the Crystal Palace in length.

" Well ! Violet, what is it? You look supremely happy this morning."

"So I am, dear." She had a way of demonstrating her affection pretty strongly, so she seized and ki ssed her friend at once; while Mrs. Colville stood to endure it with her dirty gloves and her spud held out from the clean white muslin, which she seemed to regard much more than Violet herself did. " So I am, dear Mrs. Colville. I've no work to do for a month : no horrid lessons, or anything ; and I'm come to ask you to do something for me."

Mrs. Colville laughed at her notion of happiness. " Well, what is it?"

" Have you an invitation to go to Lady Clara Barrington's pic-nic at St. Hilda's Mount on Wednesday?"

"Yes : I had it last night: and that just reminds me that I must go in and answer it." But Mrs. Colville did not stir.

"Oh ! I'm so glad:" and here she clapped her hands and laughed aloud. " Of course you'll go," she added: for it never occurred to Violet that any one could be so senseless as to refuse a pic-nic. She did not quite know how her friend had managed to sleep without having already accepted it.

"My dear child, what should Mr. Colville and I do at a pic-nic?"

"Do at a pic-nic! Why, eat cold pie, and lobster salad, and drink champagne, and run all over that beautiful place. I could sit an hour looking at that one view over the lake. Besides, we're to have music, and so many people are going. All the officers from Portbridge."

"And have no salt to my dinner: and if it should be wet, spoil my dress. I'm too old for pic-nics, Violet." Here the lady recommenced operations with the spud.

"Too old? nonsense. And there's the griffin." The griffin was Alice Colville.

"The griffin is away from home: and will go from Eastbury with the Montgomerys."

"Then you'll go for me, dear: oh! I quite forgot. Madame will not go herself, but she has given me leave to go if you will take me."

"Why didn't you tell me that before?"

"Ah! now you will go, I see, you dear old thing you." And here Violet Carloss commenced another embrace; and then sung with the sweetest voice in the world a favourite waltz, to which she danced in time.

Nobody ever resisted Violet, excepting Madame; so in this case she had her way.

"Shall I take the note for you, and send it to Lady Clara by my maid?"

"No, dear, thank you. Let it go by post."

"But then she won't get it till to-morrow."

"Well! that will be three days before the time, at any rate."

"And what are we to take?—plovers' eggs, they're easy to carry: and Stilton cheese. I am so fond of Stilton cheese, and Madame won't let me eat cheese; she says it's not 'comme il faut.' I know what that means."

"I hope so, my dear; it's time you did, and nearly time you practised it. How old are you, Violet—seventeen?"

"Not quite, yet. I shall be, next month. But what shall I do?"

"Go home, dear, and get cool, first of all: and if you'll be ready at three o'clock on Wednesday, I'll call for you in the pony-carriage."

"So I will, dear Mrs. Colville." And having given her another squeeze, she went away through the window. Frank Beauclerc was not there, so she made her way into the street, and walked home.

Mrs. Colville had a smile on her face for some minutes after she left. It was difficult to wish Violet Carloss other than she was: and yet she was so different from Mrs. Colville's standard of excellence. She was so idle, so impulsive, so ignorant, and so happy in it all! But then she was so good, so generous, so innocent, so lovable: and, after all, she wasn't seventeen.

I ought to give a description of Violet Carloss: a short one, a mere sketch. The reader must fill it up and colour it according to his taste.

The beauty of Violet was a beauty to "make

virtue shine and vice blush." Such a beauty as hers was better than all the letters of recommendation in the world. It was a beauty to which you might have bound yourself for life, with the moral certainty that it could never fade but with life itself. It could never have grown old: in her it was bound up with such enduring love. As a mother or a wife you could see that it would have absorbed all proper authority, and triumphed over the very excellences of the character: like everything earthly, it had its defect. But it would have retained, it will retain, a reflexion of its bloom long after the golden light of its spring-time or its summer has passed away.

She was verging on seventeen. She was tall and full grown beyond her years, lithe and graceful, and budding into womanhood somewhat prematurely. Her eyes were large, long, soft, of a dark grey colour: hitherto they had looked at all men with a royal indifference. The lids were full, and the veins gave amplitude to the light that quivered below them. The lashes swept her cheek with a gentle curve. Truly they were "occhi, stelle mortale." Her brow was rather low, but broad and square; and hair, the darkest auburn, waved in wrinkles over her handsome and well-shaped eyebrows.

Her nose was the most perfect feature in her face. It was small, and delicately formed: the nostrils narrow, and the bridge slightly developed nearly to the end. There is something ridiculous attached to the description of noses. All sentiment vanishes when we leave the eyes or the mouth. Why? It would have puzzled you to have answered that question had you seen that feature in Violet Carloss's face.

Her mouth was not small, but beautifully shaped. The lips were full, and of a warm bright colour: naturally parted, exhibiting at all times a glimmer of the pearly teeth within. The chin, too, was round and firm; very handsome; giving evidence of a character which the rest of her features denied. There was a fund of constancy to bear (not to forbear), through good report and evil report, which was looked for in vain in the impulsive tenderness of the rest of her face.

From childhood everybody had submitted to a gentle tyranny, which her beauty rather than her nature exercised. The facts of her case endorsed the beautiful notion of poor Keats:

The first in beauty should be first in might.

As a child, with nurses, maids, doctors, and lollypop-sellers, she was, not to make a pun, *facile princeps*, a prince of easy sway: but still a prince. Whenever she was contradicted, she threw her arms round the dissentient's neck, and covered him or her with kisses. Nobody withstood those bright round lips, and the floating auburn tresses that tumbled all over one. Nurse always gave way, for Violet laughed at her good sense, was not amenable to orders, and did as she liked, asking permission after it was over. Philosophers and old maids would have said, "Bless me! what a naughty little girl; wouldn't take her pills, and would go out without her bonnet." In fact, they did say so. Yet my friend, Dr. Bartholomew, positively idolised her; and sent her pleasant physic, because she would not take the nasty. Indeed, she kissed Dr. Bartlemy, as she called him, and desired him to send something equally good in return, or he should have no more. The gingerbread and lollypop-makers fed her from her childhood; and had encouraged a most perverted taste for Everton toffy and brandy-balls. Alas! age and indigestion always correct that.

On one person only she tried no blandishments. Madame and Violet never quarrelled, but they never loved. Madame Rosenfels thoroughly did her duty by the orphan heiress. She kept her in comfort, as far as she could in luxury; but it always seemed as if a cat was keeping watch over a mouse, for her own amusement or profit. She succumbed to nothing but a tear, and then she did so with a bad grace.

Violet was desperately idle, and, knowledge not coming in her case by intuition, not very well informed. Learning anything at all as a lesson was quite out of her way. She loved sunshine, and

kittens, and a pet dormouse; and she had a rough
terrier, who must have had a rough time of it, for
she cuddled and tormented him alternately from
morning till night. She had an excellent ear for
music, and a pretty voice. She could barely play
her own accompaniments, and, when left to herself, never did so. She reminded me of an Irish
nobleman, who never walks when he can ride, nor
rides when he can drive, nor drives when he can
be driven. She never read, and never listened
when she was being read to. She made terrible
blunders in a naïve way, at which everybody
laughed; and when any one ventured to expostu-
late with an astonished "my dear Violet!" she
stopped the exclaimant with kisses, and brought up
her face from the embrace covered with blushes
and laughter. Heavens! what a mass of smiles
the girl was. They would have redeemed the
ugliest face in Christendom. There are smiles
indicative of fifty different feelings: but vary the
smiles of Violet Carloss as you will, they all
ended in love. There was a radiance of goodness
and innocence and truth all over her, which defied

ill nature, and set even the justest reproof at nought.

Now do not suppose that I am an advocate for this sort of young person. Forfend it, Heaven! The most dangerous of implements in the hands of society is a dear, lovable creature that nobody has courage to correct. She upsets all principles of education and training, gives very little chance to the theorists, and none whatever to the practical. I only tell you what she was. She had thousands of faults. Was always doing or saying injudicious things; only nobody regarded them as such from her. She was quite an irresponsible agent: just as much so as a pet kitten would have been. I ought, too, to reconcile a curious anomaly in her character in these days of universal "ologies" and "isms." She neither knew nor cared where the Achelous was: had most eccentric notions of Calcutta, Madras, and Bombay, of which she judged, poor child! by London, Liverpool, and Manchester as to distance: and had never heard that Peter the Great and Charles the

Twelfth were contemporaries : yet she was a most amusing companion, said very excellent things occasionally, and delighted in the *Times* newspaper. She peopled the village with organ-grinders and beggars by the indiscriminate alms that she gave, and horrified the philanthropists by denouncing the union workhouse.

Such was the heroine of my story.

CHAPTER VIII.

A NEW ACQUAINTANCE.

Mystery magnifies danger, as a fog the sun.

THE pupil-room at Harry Colville's looked on to the turnpike-road: and as Lymmersfield was a grand public thoroughfare for all the surrounding neighbourhood to the metropolis, it was a favourite resort for the candidates for examination. There they stood at the receipt of custom, either of the two windows, and criticised carriages, dog-carts, broughams, and pony-chairs on their road to the railway station.

From nine to ten was the most popular hour for

this diversion, when they were supposed to be preparing their work, and when the street was alive
with the patrons of the daily-bread trains which
accommodated learned serjeants, rising counsel,
topping attorneys, Stock Exchange men, and City
tradesmen on their way from their villas to their
various occupations.

The room of which we speak had few pecu-
liarities worth mentioning. Two-thirds of the wall
was devoted to books, and the rest was occupied
by windows and doors. There was a large table
in the middle: about ten strong serviceable chairs,
and there was a fireplace, of course not lighted,
though laid even in the middle of July, ready for
an emergency. Colville's arm-chair occupied one
corner, and by its side was a small table, on
which were writing materials, and a book or two:
Arnold's "Thucydides" and Aristotle's "Ethics."
On the larger table were some works more popular
with the present occupants of the study. Some
short cuts to a "satisfactory result," known under
the popularly fallacious name of "knowledge;" as

Chepmell's "History," Anthon's "Cæsar" and "Homer," and all the direct commission examination papers of the last three years. Against the wall was a black board, on which in chalk were the two sides of a simple equation, and a figure of the forty-seventh proposition of the first book of Euclid.

Its present occupants were four boys, who called themselves men. They would have been so, if seventeen or eighteen summers, capacious pockets, neat boots, well-cut clothes, and considerable self-sufficiency, gave any sort of claim to the distinction. Two of them were from Eton, one from Harrow, the fourth was from a private establishment conducted on the modern system; he had a little more modesty, but not more knowledge than the rest.

Bentley stood with his back to the unlighted fireplace, leaning against the mantelpiece, with his hands buried fathom-deep in his pockets. He was staring out of window: and from his occasional remarks there was plenty to stare at.

" There goes Manning in his brougham. What the d—l does he wear a white choker for? Lawyers have no business with white chokers; only waiters and parsons."

" But he's a churchwarden," said Standish, the private school pupil, whose views were less *prononcés* than those of his companion : " besides, just look at the lot of money he gave to the new church."

" And just look at the poor devils of clients he took it out of. I should like to see them : there's nothing like justice in this world, is there, Gorsehampton ? "

Lord Gorsehampton was reading, or trying to read ; but he looked up, and said, " No : nothing at all like it : somebody's always making a row about something or other."

" There goes Lady Clara Barrington. What a capital judge of a horse Barrington is."

" Who says so ? " said young Pitt, late of the fifth form at Harrow, who, being the son of a master of hounds, thought this an incursion on his especial prerogative : besides, he was fond of taking down Bentley, who, being in a like position, gave himself airs, and was Eton.

"Who says so?—why, why, everybody says so!" rejoined Bentley.

" What, all the people about here ? "

" Yes, everybody ! "

" Ah ! then, it can't be true : for I've heard you say a hundred times nobody knows anything about a horse here ; so everybody's judgment can't be worth much."

"But he is a very good judge," said Lord Gorschampton, " and always drives and rides capital cattle."

" I didn't say he wasn't. I only asked who said so ; and Bentley said a great many people who didn't know anything about it. Are you going to the pic-nic at St. Hilda's Mount, Gorschampton ?" inquired Bentley, after a pause.

" Not if I know it. When is it ? "

" To-morrow : didn't you have a ticket ? "

" Yes," said the indolent young aristocrat ;

"Lady Clara said something about it, but I forgot it. Who's going?"

"Why, the Montgomerys, and the Barkers, and the Trefusis, and the officers from Portbridge, and I think I shall go."

"Then I certainly shall not," said Carr. "I shall go on the river."

"What difference can my going make to you, I should like to know?" said Bentley, who was getting a little savage.

"We should have to come back together, and the strength of your tobacco, with the windows up, is quite insufferable." Here the rest of them laughed so cheerfully, that Bentley was obliged to assume good humour. So he asked whether Beauclerc was going.

"Of course he is," said Standish.

"Why of course? I don't see it."

"He's spooney on that pretty girl, Violet Carloss, and she's going: I heard Mrs. Colville tell the governor so."

"What's your idea of being spooney, Stand-

L 2

ish?" said Lord Gorschampton: "I should be
curious to see Beauclerc in that state. What
makes you think Beauclerc is spooney on Violet
Carloss?"

"Well, I'll tell you. He walked up to their
house with them on Sunday after church, and it's
more than half a mile out of the way: besides, I
saw him carrying her prayer-book. If you don't
call that being spooney, I should just like to know
your idea of it."

"I quite agree with you, my dear fellow," said
Gorschampton. "I never knew a stronger case.
I dare say the pic-nic will be good fun. I think
I shall go, if it's not too hot. Let's all go: we
can get a fly."

Just at this point of this animated discussion
the study door opened, and Beauclerc came in.

"Beauclerc, they say you're going to Lady
Clara's pic-nic. She's given a sort of invite to
the house, and some of us think of going."

"So much the better. The more the merrier,"
said Frank.

"Will you join us? We want something to go in: a fly, or a phaeton, or an omnibus. We must have two horses: it's such a deuce of a pull to the top of the mount."

"I can't go with you fellows: for I dine and sleep at Ashdale the day before, and I shall drive from there."

"Is that Lord Ashdale's place?" asked Pitt.

"Yes: he's a cousin of mine, and Fred Ashdale is quartered at Portbridge just now. Do you know him?"

"We were at Eton at the same dame's, and in the same form a good part of the time. What a capital fellow he is!"

"I think if you spoke to Colville or Mrs. Colville, you might all go together in Faulkner's 'bus: she has to take Miss Carloss." Saying which, he left the room, whistling an air from the Trovatore.

"I say, Bentley, I don't think he's so very spooney, after all," said his Lordship. "You might cut him out, if you tried hard."

"I don't think he'll die of it this time, at all events," said another. "However, I vote we propose it to the governor, and see what he says."

"I recollect now, I heard of Frank Beauclerc being at Ashdale's for his winter holidays. Lord Ashdale was master of the hounds last season, and there was an account of an extraordinary run, which no one saw excepting Lord Ashdale himself and Beauclerc. I'd no idea it was the same."

"By Jove!" said Pitt, "he ought to be patronised."

"He don't look to me as if he would stand much patronage. It might spoil him, Pitt," said Lord Gorsehampton, from the middle of a proposition. In truth, I think his Lordship, with all his inexperience, was right. Just then Colville entered the room. "Will you join us, sir, in an omnibus to go to Lady Clara's pic-nic?"

"Yes," said Mr. Colville. "I suppose I must go, if you all go."

"Then that's five of us," said Lord Gorse-hampton. "I'll order the 'bus."

"Yes, there'll be plenty of room," replied their tutor. "Miss Carloss and Mrs. Colville are going to drive in the pony-chair."

The faces of more than one of the party were exceedingly blank. Whether a natural taste for ladies' society had led to the proposition, or an especial fancy for these two in particular, I cannot say. At all events, it was too late to retract; so, instead of a phaeton or a fly, and a plentiful supply of tobacco, they were condemned to the company of the Rev. Harry Colville and an omnibus : and very good company it was, too. "By Jove! look at Madame; she's off to town!"

Time had dealt leniently with Madame Rosen-fels since we were last in her company. She was still as good-looking as ever : well preserved : and handsomely dressed : her jewellery, although it was morning, was remarkably good, and, if plen-tiful, selected with much care as to its value and propriety. It was massive, and of the Italian type: and the gems among it were rare and of the finest water. Her straight, cleanly-cut features were the least likely to have suffered from time. With the exception of a little hardness, there was no alteration in thirteen years.

Why was Madame still a widow? Everybody asked the question, but no one answered it satisfactorily: and no man solved it by cutting the Gordian knot.

Madame Rosenfels was ambitious. That's the truth. Like many clever women, she felt her power, and intended greater things than common. There was another *pourquoi* in the case. For some reason or other, she affected mystery or concealment. Now, Madame was just the person to have won her way in a crowd. Lymmersfield, a picturesque, quasi-suburban village, was neither far enough off from, nor near enough to, London to make it available as a matrimonial market in her sense of the term. The people were migratory, the men especially: and they lived on the railroad. A widow does most mischief in the morning; the evening is the time for the fire-flies to exhibit.

Besides, for the present, what more was to be got than she already possessed? A comfortable home, and some luxuries : the management of somebody else's money almost without control : to be exchanged for an uncertainty. She had put herself down at a thousand a year, and a man whom she could profess to love or to admire; and Lymmersfield had not yet presented her with the opportunity.

Lymmersfield was a mistake. Brighton, Bath, Cheltenham, Malvern even, might have done: and sometimes she thought of giving them a trial. One consideration prevented it.

Immediately previous to the death of Major Carloss he had become acquainted, by some ordinary communication, with the Colvilles' residence at Lymmersfield. A correspondence ensued. Harry Colville had been an intimate friend of some of the Major's family, and at the Major's death he found himself associated, to a certain extent, in the guardianship of Violet and her property. It

was clear that if Madame Rosenfels changed her
name again, Violet would seek a home with the
Colvilles. She was not empowered to do so, so
long as Madame, her mother's earliest friend, had
an independent and undivided one to offer.

Madame was extravagant : personally so rather
than otherwise. Handsome women frequently are
so without intending it. The previous co-guar-
dian, General Fletcher, who was now dead, had
been a singularly apathetic and easy-going person.
He had been put to some trouble (he cared nothing for expense) about a trumpery three hundred pounds which was unaccounted for. Madame's oratory and eyelashes were too much for
him, and he resigned the inquiry and the guardianship together. From that time real responsibility rested only with Madame, who, however, for
her credit's sake, suggested some mutual friend
as a coadjutor. Unprotected females are fond of
listening to advice, as they would pay for a pre-
scription, without much idea of taking it.

The Major was singularly unlucky in his choice once more. Harry Colville had a dozen irons in the fire, and the only thing of which he knew absolutely nothing was money. His wife managed his house, signed his cheques, and paid his bills: presenting him with what he wanted. It was usually sixpence to pay the turnpike, and not that when she was with him. As to suspicions of other people's money matters going wrong, that never crossed his brain.

Adelaide Rosenfels sat in her chaise longue of the most comfortable fashion, looking out on a small but well-kept lawn. She was reading a French novel, for she liked her luxuries; and we need not venture upon classing that with the necessaries of life. Some women declare they cannot live without singing-birds and scarlet geraniums, without Pivet's gloves, or Melnotte's boots, a French maid, or a Dutch poodle: we presume they have never tried. Madame said the same of French romances. Whether they consoled her for the omission of good, or nerved her for the commission of evil, I cannot tell.

Violet Carloss was gone into the village to buy some tarlatan, to beg some exotics which she could not buy, and to call upon a poor old woman, whose cow had died in the night in full milk. Madame had the house to herself.

The door opened, and a very respectable-looking woman of middle age, and presenting the appearance of a high class of servant, brought in a note on a waiter, adding, "There's somebody waiting to see you, ma'am. The person who brought that note."

Madame Rosenfels did as many do on a hot day; instead of looking inside of the letter, she turned it upside down three or four times, inspecting the writing and the seal minutely, and then replied to her servant:

" Who is it, and what does he want? "

" I don't know, ma'am. It's a woman—a woman of colour." Madame Rosenfels was not a woman of colour at any time : at that moment less so than usual: but in a second the blood returned to her face with too great violence, and she became conscious of a very unusual blush upon her usually pale clear face.

" Tell her to sit down, and I will see her immediately."

The letter was one of mere recommendation from the lawyer who had been employed in Miss Carloss's affairs when necessary. It mentioned the arrival from India of a person who had inquired her address, and, being no great proficient in our language, had begged a letter in case of need.

And yet Madame Rosenfels felt very uncomfortable.

The firm of Fleecehall and Shearham was a most respectable firm. Fleecehall did the business: Shearham was the man of pleasure, and made himself agreeable to the clients. He had once cast his eyes on Madame Rosenfels. It was before he knew the exact extent of her income and whence she derived it. He had since been grateful for the rejection, but remained a devoted admirer.

Madame went up-stairs, and came down again refreshed. Looking indeed more than herself: when the "woman of colour" presented herself at the door.

"Baba!" The surprise on Madame's part was well acted.

"Madame!" Such were the exclamations; and then followed a series of natural questions, such as might be expected between mistress and maid who had not met for thirteen years.

"Baba, you are a little changed. You don't look well." And she gave her a chair.

"Et vous, Madame, and you so well." Then the conversation continued in French, for Baba was a French Indian: and had been living long in Pondicherry with a French family: doubtless a useful woman, who made a pillau out of as little as most people, and dressed the young ladies' hair equally well. "And my little girl, Madame——?"

"Yes—your little girl is become a great beauty; you shall see her. Ah! here she comes: Violet dear: here's Nurse Baba come all the way from

India to see you." Nurse Baba's features exhibited considerable surprise at something.

Violet Carloss was delighted to see her nurse of whom she had heard not much : she knew that a nurse had come over with her and her little cousin ; but that was all. She had forgotten the cousin and the nurse too.

Baba's conversation in the servants' apartments was in praise of Miss Carloss. Beyond that it was difficult to get. She seemed mightily puzzled by the name, and repeated "Violet!" "Violet!" to herself several times over. "Par hasard," said she, in very unintelligible English, "was it Miss Marguerite."

Before Baba returned to town she had another interview with Madame Rosenfels. Violet was away from home during the time.

"And what are you going to do with yourself—stop in England?" said Madame.

"It is so triste, Madame. And now I get old I must go to France or India. I have friends in both."

"Certainly. It is triste. Can I be of assistance to you? I shall be delighted if I can find any situation that would be of service to you on the Continent, or in India. Here it is scarcely probable that I shall be able to serve you."

She was lavish of her thanks. "Madame was always so kind."

"And Miss Marguerite? Shall I see her again?" inquired the woman.

"Margaret: ah! nurse, you forget. Poor little thing. We shall all see her again."

Madame was not a religious character; but she had her belief, and it was a creditable and consolatory one in this respect. So thought Baba.

"Ah! Miss Violet, of course, but——" And here ensued a pause, until the old Indian began muttering the two names, as if balancing their value.

"Baba! what are you talking about? Come with me. I have something to show you in my wardrobe. Margaret left a little present behind for those who were kind to her in her last illness."

Madame led the Indian, still exhibiting some signs of astonishment, into a luxuriously furnished bedroom. From a small chest of drawers, she unlocked and drew out the bottom one of all. It contained much female gear, ribbons, embroidery, lappets of point lace, and other gauze-like and gossamer articles of adornment. From one corner Madame drew forth several baby dresses rolled up roughly, but of costly work and materials. On each and all was marked the name of "Margaret."

"There, Baba, are the little frocks and caps; and there's one with Brussels lace on it that we have put by for you: you must take the mark out when you have time." Baba looked pleased but puzzled. "And there was a little present, too, to be given to you, which will be still more useful, I hope, and help you to get back to India." Saying which, the graceful Madame Rosenfels slipped a note into the hand of her old nurse, which sounded crisper and looked less soiled than might have been expected from the date of the legacy.

Baba was a French East Indian. Could she

contradict so clever and so excellent a woman as
Madame? So she went up to London from the
Lymmersfield station; and it gave her an hour to
think what an old imbecile she had become in a
dozen years, before her friends met her and carried
her off from the curious gaze of the travelling
public.

CHAPTER IX.

A PIC-NIC.

Now comes a call, that conquers all resistance.
COLLINS.

"WHERE are you going, Beauclerc?" said
Pitt, emitting a cloud of Cavendish and bird's-
eye out of his mouth, on the morning before the
pic-nic, emerging from the greenhouse after breakfast, where he had been, as he said, improving
the plants.

"I'm going to dinner at Ashdale, by train, to-
day; and I shall meet you all at St. Hilda's
Mount to-morrow. How do you go?"

"Oh! such a sell: Colville offered to share the 'bus with us, so of course we agreed; and then he let out that Violet Carloss was going in the pony-chair."

"I don't see what difference that could make to you?" said Frank, doggedly.

"Don't you. Why, we only wanted to go for the fun of going with her, you know."

"Really; whose notion is that?"

"Bentley's, to be sure. Didn't you know he's tremendous sweet on her? That's why he smells so awfully of scent—jockey-club, I think it is: and don't you see how particular he is about his back hair? He sits just before her and Madame What's-her-name in church," said Pitt.

"But I thought he didn't know them."

"No more he does much. But she comes to Colville's very often, and he's taken to going into the drawing-room lately of an evening: so Mrs. Colville patronises him. He has just discovered that he is exceedingly fond of Beethoven."

"And why don't you go into the drawing-room

too, instead of going up to that villanous tap at the Fox and Hounds?"

"Oh! hang that! there's nothing to do there excepting to read, or hear the griffin play and sing; besides, I know all her songs." The Griffin sang and played very well, notwithstanding.

"Where are you going now, Pitt? I'm going up here to get a dog-collar for Pixie."

"And I'm going to have some beer before lecture." With that they parted : their roads lying as widely apart as their inclinations.

If ever there was a mistake in the educational system, it is in the necessity (for it is a necessity) for private preparation for competitive examination. If Eton and Harrow do nothing more, they do insist upon discipline : they do give authority for the punishment of faults : they practically keep pipes and beer without the limits of discovery : there is no avowed impunity for them : and they have some check upon a love of low company. There are conscientious men in the world who will look after the idlers entrusted to them; who see a duty beyond the reigns of the kings of England, or the solution of an equation. But it requires a clever tactician to keep the twig straight just under the circumstances and at the time it is most given to bend.

Colville had had his fair share of experience, and he found the cunning of the serpent as useful as the innocence of the dove.

The morning of Wednesday, the — of July, was as bright and lovely as mornings in July frequently are. A curling vapour, through which the sun's rays were penetrating, bespoke certain heat. The dew hung yet upon the flowers, for not a cloud had returned her radiating warmth to the earth, when she poured it forth through the still hours of the night. It bade fair to be a day for a pic-nic, without alloy.

Some people dislike pic-nics. I do not venture to give an opinion either way. They are provoking and provocative. Provoking in an English climate, as throwing a doubt over the certainty of their fulfilment: provocative of love and indigestion ; both which states of being should be entered upon with great consideration. I suit my views to my company; and, as the father of a large family, have plenty of exercise for my ingenuity.

Barrington could not endure them. "For a man who could afford a Turkey carpet, a mahogany table, good claret, and an attentive butler, to dine on wet grass or hot turf, with half-flat claret, after laying his own cloth, and uncorking his own champagne, is preposterous — positively preposterous, Clara!" Lady Clara was of a different opinion. She thought nothing so charming as a dinner at St. Hilda's Mount: true, it was but six miles from Lymmersfield Park, and she could have gone there every day; but then she never did, excepting on these occasions. She liked getting wet, by way of a change: ordinary life was dry enough in all conscience. She preferred her claret a little flat *sometimes*, and she should have plenty of people to wait upon her. Barrington, who was a good-looking, good-tempered swell, ex-captain of the — Life Guards, would ride up in the cool of the day, if he could find it, and return to an eight o'clock dinner. The views were beautiful, and they meant to go on the lake.

Lady Clara was like most women who are young and pretty: especially when they are so unfortunate as to have no domestic troubles or incumbrances. She liked pleasure; admiration; *abandon*: it was something different from the Belgravian pattern of which she had just undergone six weeks' probation. Rotten Row was charming then; but her taste was pure enough to prefer St. Hilda's now.

I find all men, of a certain age, something like Barrington. Love-making, especially in other people, gives us very little satisfaction. We have most of us seen a fine country or two, and prefer Leicestershire: and have had so many bad dinners that we are disinclined to add to the number. A grey beard at a pic-nic ought to wag with astonishment at finding itself there.

Of one young lady the enjoyment was likely to

be as unmistakable as it was pure. Violet Carloss
was coming out to-day. Her notion of the material world was Lady Clara, on the top of St.
Hilda's Mount, making a salad, and thirty people
in charming costumes waiting to partake of it.
The background was grouped with blue sky,
water, trees, birds, and fishing-boats; and the
middle distance with mail-phaetons, open ba-
rouches, and pony-carriages. Her notion of the
moral world was an universal philanthropy, which
diminished or increased irrationally towards certain persons without reference to anything but her
own free will. It should be observed that in this
moral thermometer the mercury in Violet had
never yet reached freezing point, while it was
prepared to ascend to any height whatever.

Poor child! how very happy she was by nature
intended to be! She had something to learn in
which dulness of comprehension is a great
blessing.

She has to learn that the world is not all sunshine and flowers; that woman can be trea-

cherous, man self-interested ; that our best feelings
may be made the severest instruments of our tor-
ture : that hypocrisy is the homage that vice
pays to virtue : that the world is made up of
tinsel. She has to learn that the warmth of a
caress is no criterion of its honesty; that heat on
the surface, like blood from the heart, leaves an
icicle within. To be sure the purchase of this
experience will be sweet enough : its possession—
bitter. Her lesson will be conned in a world of
appearances : and, on a path strewed with flowers,
poor Violet, like others, must pick up her thorns.
And then she has something more to discover :
that adversity has its merits—that she must be
evil thought of, or spoken of, when blameless ;
that she must suffer for the short-comings of
others ; and that " the fathers have eaten sour
grapes, and the children's teeth are set on edge."
Then she will know, to her own profit, that she
may look inwardly for consolation, and that she
will find it when her whole and absolute dependence is upon God.

By five o'clock the last carriage had reached St. Hilda's Mount.

"And now what shall we do?" said Lady Clara, charmingly dressed, in the lightest of summer finery, and looking the picture of English good humour and enjoyment. "What shall we do? Lunch first, or walk to the ruins, or go on the water?"

"Lunch first, Lady Clara, by all means : it will give us an appetite for sight-seeing." Saying which, the gallant Colonel Twigg, throwing his rein to his servant, dismounted, and offered his hand to her ladyship. She came down from a well-appointed barouche; and her two sisters, equally splendid, but more youthful in costume, followed her.

" Violet, you must come and sit by me. Where's Madame? Not come? Not come to my pic-nic? Well, we must do without her. And who did you come with?"

" With Mrs. Colville. Madame Rosenfels is not very well; and said I was to say everything

most kind to you for her. She goes out so
seldom." The fact is, that Madame had refused
for both, originally; but had been over-persuaded
by her ladyship's eloquence: so she sent Violet
as a compromise.

Then the hampers were made to descend from
their places on the carriage: and Captain Slow-
come turned up his shirt-sleeves and commenced
a search in the straw. Glorious long-necked
bottles were extracted. Ice was discovered: a
piece of which, *au naturel*, Lady Sarah Slaughter-
man appropriated at once, staining her gloves and
spoiling her bonnet-strings.

" Sarah, dear !" said Lady Clara, reprovingly.

" Can't help it, dear; that carriage of yours is
like an oven. Just look at me, Captain Ashdale"
(that languid individual had just arrived); " don't
I look dreadful ? "

" Terrible indeed, Lady Sarah. Apply to my
friend Boldover here ; he's the coolest hand I've
ever known." Lady Sarah looked up, and there
recognised an old acquaintance in the phaeton.

" Major Boldover : now pray make yourself

useful. Come down and dress the salad. Where did you come from?" Boldover obeyed, and answered, in one breath :

"I came from Ireland last night." Here the Major alighted from the phaeton, and, having made a comprehensive sort of bow, seized a cucumber in his left hand. "How can I cut it without 'ere a knife?" said the Major, looking round in despair : "and——" But no one waited for the conclusion.

"A knife? Here's a knife." And Major Boldover was soon in the middle of his performance, after a personal introduction to Lady Clara.

"My dear Mrs. Colville, give me the pepper," said Lady Clara; and she proceeded to assist the Major. "Oh! look at the wasps : I'm sure there's a nest."

"Where's the gunpowder?" said the Major, dropping the rest of the cucumber.

"Gunpowder : what's the use of gunpowder?"

"Blow up the nest." And all the young ladies jumped up.

"But there is none, unless you send to the barracks at Portbridge."

"Then let's have some boiling water. We'll soon settle them."

"Let them settle themselves," said Frank Beauclerc.

Major Boldover looked up. "Very good: who is that young man, Ashdale?"

"That's a cousin of mine. How do, Beauclerc? By Jove, where are you? I didn't know you were here." Then the two fraternised as cousins should do, and they sat down together and had some mutual confidences.

"So you are promised a vacancy in ours. When's the exam.?" inquired Frederick Ashdale, who had come from the barracks.

"Next month."

"All right, I suppose? Because, you know, they want a fellow to know something, I can tell you. Arithmetic and all that sort of thing. I was very nearly floored; and they're deuced particular about the spelling."

Frank thought he might do.

"Lady Clara, is the champagne iced yet?"

"No, Fred; all the ice has melted. Where's the salt?"

"Here's the salt, my lady," said Bentley, in a very modest tone of voice. He was not half the man he appeared to be in the Fox and Hounds tap, when he was chaffing the Lymmersfield butcher about the trotting pony. My lady and her friends rather awed him.

"Lord Gorsehampton, may I trouble you to cut that cherry tart? Violet, you don't eat anything. Mrs. Colville, I hope Violet hasn't been lunching with you." Lady Clara did not wait for an answer, but went on assiduously taking care of her guests.

"Walker, where's the claret?" That dignified functionary condescended to look surprised.

"Please, my lady, I rather think—I'm afraid—yes, my lady." Here Walker buried his head in all parts of the barouche, and at last admitted that it had been forgotten.

The faces were blank of those who heard the

announcement: but young Caradoc allayed all apprehension by ordering his groom to unpack the hamper behind him. Claret was produced in abundance.

"Evelyn?" Miss Ashdale, a pretty girl in golden bands and a white lace bonnet, looked up from a flirtation with Cornet Rathbone. "When is the Goodwood meeting? Isn't it late this year?"

"Yes, dear; it's a movable feast. It depends upon Easter."

"Of course you go?"

"Yes, dear. Papa has a horse entered. He ran a very good trial; only we don't talk about it, you know."

Here the Barracks at Portbridge laughed solemnly, and Major Boldover said: "Certainly not: quite right, Miss Ashdale; keep it among friends." This was the Major's first introduction to that young lady; but people soon become intimate at a pic-nic; at least, people like Major Boldover.

It is not the quantity of the meat, but the cheerfulness of the guests which make a feast, says somebody : and as the table was pretty well cleared, the ladies began to move. The wasps had peaceable possession of the viands, and Captain Ashdale had began to fumble with his cigar-case, when Barrington arrived. He was a tall, good-looking man, and displayed to perfection the Newmarket hack which he had ridden up the hill.

" Any claret-cup left ?" said he, after the first salutations. " There always is a little ;" so he drank, and then spoke to Fred Ashdale.

"Isn't there a man of the name of Beauclerc here ? He's reading with Colville, and I want to ask him to come to our house."

" Yes, here he is : he's a cousin of mine. Beauclerc." Frank was close by, and he was soon in conversation with Captain Barrington.

" Oh ! Miss Montgomery, I'm so glad you came. Is your sister here ?"

" She was a minute ago. They're gone towards the cottage to order tea to be ready, when we come back from the lake."

" The lake ? Have you got the boats ? That's

capital. Just take hold of my hack, will you?"
and he surrendered his horse to one of the servants.
"Oh, Miss Carloss, I hear Madame wouldn't come;
how sorry I am! Lady Clara says she could have
given you a seat with her, if she had but known in
time."

"Thanks, Captain Barrington, it's very kind of
Lady Clara. Mrs. Colville brought me."

"And is Mr. Colville come? It is not much in
his way."

"Yes, he's here somewhere." Colville had be-
taken himself to a cigar in a more retired corner of
the hill.

Having ascertained that tea was to be had in a
couple of hours, the ladies and gentlemen paired
off, as best they might. Violet fell to the lot of
Cornet Caradoc, and Frank Beauclerc took possession of Evelyn Ashdale. Barrington took charge
of old Lady Ashdale, who had chaperoned her
daughter, and in a few minutes they all met at one
of the numerous points of view to be found on St.
Hilda's Mount.

The old ruined monastery at the foot of the hill,
near the water, was a picturesque object. It was a
complete ruin, but retaining internally the divisions
of kitchen, refectory, and the other component
parts of a large religious house. It was covered
with ivy, and the gnarled and twisted roots helped
to support the crumbling windows and delicate
tracery of the dormitories, which were easily dis-
cernible from the interior. Dick Tinteman, when
studying manfully against the adverse criticism
and invidious hanging of the Committee of the
R.A. Society, has rendered its beauties familiar
to all who saw that famous picture—and who did
not see it?—known as "The Hand of Time." I am
under great obligations to Dick, and so is the
reader : he has saved us both a great deal of
trouble.

Of course some of Lady Clara's party had never
seen it before, so that it made an admirable point
after the splendid view from the top of the hill had
been duly eulogised. Not that the one is to compare in our opinion with the other. A fine view,

of vast extent, is a grand thing. It appeals to the best feelings. The works of nature extending before us lift us from the earth, and we bless so lavish a hand which has spread a feast to be enjoyed by all. Dotted here and there are the works of man : the churches, the hamlets, villages, towns, for which the infinite framework of the great Artist was designed. And we don't come down again, as in daily life, to the sordid passions, the hardships, the selfishness, of our fellow-creatures : we see his humble trusts, his honest labour, his industry, his heaven-born powers, and we thank God that He has made us as near Him as we are. A ruin ! a reverend history of a time gone by, good or bad, as it may be.

Nature is the true object of antiquarian research. Its hills, its glades, rocks, waterfalls, the teeming earth, the silently flowing streams, these put to the test the true value of antiquity. I wonder how many thousands of years they took to form, how many they have endured without perceptible change, and how many they will yet serve to the happiness, enjoyment, and necessities of the human race.

"What an enormous place!" said Miss Montgomery. "How charming to people it, dear Lady Ashdale, with the tenants of——"

"Good Heavens, my dear, what a family!" replied the old lady. I think, by a little twinkle of the eye, Lady Ashdale was not so obtuse as she pretended to be : but the answer made Miss Montgomery less poetical for the time.

"Who built this place, Mr. Colville?" inquired Lady Ashdale.

"I don't know who built it, but I know who despoiled it, Lady Ashdale."

"Do you, sir? then be good enough to tell us."

"An ancestor of Lord Ashdale. Is not St. Hilda's vicarage in your gift, my lady?"

"In Lord Ashdale's it is. But I don't see what that has to do with the old monastery."

"When Lord Ashdale's ancestor turned out the monks, he got the great tithes, and we got a poor-

law to supply the place of its charities.   This was
one of the largest."

"And therefore did the most good," said the old
lady, stoutly.

"According to your ancestor's reading, it did
the most harm."

"It kept the poor in bread and cheese, Mr. Colville."

"And encouraged them to beg for it, my lady :
but you ought not to defend the system."

While this discussion had been going on, the
couples had separated, or were improving the occasion, each according to taste, capacity, or inclination ; which are different in different men.

"Rum old fellows, those monks, Miss Ashdale,"
said Major Boldover.

"Scarcely the view I should take of them,"
said the young lady, with a rather satirical smile.
Miss Ashdale had been raised in Belgravia, and
admired Father Eustace, who approached that
condition of life as far as his judicious diocesan
would allow.

"I say, Barrington, this must have been the stable," said Caradoc, pointing to some iron rings which had been driven into the wall.

"Oh! those fellows never hunted, you may depend upon it."

"Why not? The whole place belonged to them: and there were plenty of deer."

"Ask Miss Carloss," says Captain Barrington; "she knows a great deal better than I do."

"Indeed, I don't know anything: I always ask Madame. Here's Mr. Beauclerc; perhaps he knows." And they repeated the inquiry: a harmless but foolish one. Barrington joined her: Caradoc was puzzled, and began to consider the question rather seriously.

"Charming style!" said a young gentleman, with unexceptionable boots and a lisp, from the barracks, pointing to a half-ruined window. "What a pity Cromwell and those sort of fellows destroyed everything, Lady Emily."

Lady Emily, being only lately out of the schoolroom, asked, "Which Cromwell?"

"Aha! that's good: now you know you're chaffing, Lady Emily." By this time, as the ruins covered some acres, the company did the same. The young ones seeming to discover much beautiful tracery in out-of-the-way corners, cool spots in retired nooks, and to be enthusiastically devoted to the examination of botanical specimens on the walls. Somebody, however, mentioned the boats, and they began to stroll that way.

CHAPTER X.

THE BOATING PARTY.

She floats upon the river—of his thoughts.
LONGFELLOW.

AT that moment it became apparent that Lady Clara and her company were not quite alone in the ruins. A wayworn-looking figure, clad in a pair of soldier's trousers and a frock-coat, and bearing some marks of military character about him, seemed to come from no one knew where. He had been asleep in the chapel, and now, seeing so many good-looking people around him, bethought himself of the probability of taxing their liberality.

There was something about the man that did not look like ordinary pauperism. He blushed as he touched his hat: and nothing but a sad and petitioning expression of the face demanded an alms. But who was to stop at a moment like this? "An old soldier, Miss Ashdale; I'm too old a soldier for that," said Colonel Twigg. "Cool sort of hand that," said the Irish Major, who had just come from a country where poverty assumes a more commanding aspect, and demands your purse at the end of a shillelagh. "How's a fellow in lemon-coloured kids to get at a sixpence, I should like to know; at least not if they fit as they should. Besides, this sort of thing is quite a tax. I don't think the keepers ought to allow these men about." · Yes! it is a tax indeed that Heaven lays upon all men, and good citizens of that country will not refuse to pay it.

Barrington threw him sixpence, and then looked very much ashamed of himself, and followed Lady Clara towards the water. Violet Carloss was not comfortable with her companion; and as they went on talking and laughing, she called Frank Beauclerc to her side.

"Frank, do me a favour. Turn back to the ruin. I have left something behind that I want to look at again."

"Certainly. What's that?"

"It's that old soldier: he said he had been in India."

"Did he? I didn't hear him." And Frank Beauclerc seemed as indifferent as the rest to the fact, excepting that it belonged to Violet.

"Yes! he did. I heard him talking about all sorts of 'bads.' You know all the Indian names in the geography end in 'bad.' There's Hydrabad, and Allahabad, and I don't know how many. I want just to give him a shilling, and I daren't do it with all those people—so don't you tell."

"Not I, Violet." Frank seemed to have fallen into the Christian name very well, for a few weeks' practice only. "Not I: but if you want to relieve all the Indian impostors of the day, you should have a tent on the steps of the Oriental

in Hanover-square. There a real Sepoy sweeps
the crossing, and a high-class Brahmin sells tame
adders at the door."

Violet Carloss had no objection to listen to her
conductor, if he only allowed her to do as she
liked: and as she did that, without any longer
conference than to know that the object of her
charity had been discharged from the Indian
army, and was making his way to Portbridge (so
he said, at least, and an old soldier's word is as
good as his bond; in this case quite as good), she
did not detain him long. "Now, Violet, suppose
we go down to the boat."

"Violet," said the old soldier to himself. "I
knew a Violet once, a little Violet. It has found
a safer shelter and a better garden than any on
earth." Then he bethought him of following to
the lake. Mayhap he might be of service, bless
her sweet face, and earn another shilling or
two, too.

I cannot say that Violet had any of those extraordinary presentiments of danger so common in

unreal life when she went down to the water. It
would be wrong to doubt those who assert that
they are common. Still, under the circumstances,
why do they go? Certainly Violet knew nothing
about what was to happen, or she would not have
gone.

There were two boats on the lake. One was a
good family tub: useful for elderly ladies or
timid young ones, and fishing parties. The other
was an outrigger, formerly the property of the
Honourable Fred Ashdale, when he indulged in
condition and blisters. He had not done so of
late years; but the boat remained, a temptation to
the unwary, a delusion to the confident.

The big boat was soon manned; Colonel Twigg
was assiduous in handing in the ladies and in
taking his own seat by the side of Lady Clara
Barrington. Colville's pupils were about to render
themselves useful as well as ornamental. Some
had escaped in quest of more delightful scenery,
under an engagement to meet at the cottage at
eight o'clock. Two or three young ladies still

remained on the margin of the lake, and the *cavalieri serventi* were offering their services to give them, one at a time, a little row. "Mind and sit quietly," said Fred Ashdale, "and there's no danger." "The middle of the boat, Miss Montgomery: don't step on one side, or you'll go through."

"I don't like it at all," said that young lady, looking at her crinoline, which was undoubtedly beyond the capacity of a cranky outrigger.

"Let's have a turn alone first;" and Frank Beauclerc took off his coat and seated himself amidships, dropping his skulls lightly into the water, after laying the boat's head from the shore.

After taking a sweep or two across the water, Frank returned to the shore. Ladies are proverbially impatient, and his apparent confidence in his own abilities furnished the same virtue in the others. Miss Montgomery thought it would do. Violet had no doubts, and Evelyn Ashdale had been in it hundreds of times: but now she was heavier, she knew. "Not much," says her brother.

"Then you skull me, Fred." "Nonsense; Beauclerc skulls better than I do." The young lady
thought she might venture, if Mr. Beauclerc was
quite certain it wouldn't capsize. Mr. Beauclerc
was certain : at least, it depended on the lady. In
another minute Miss Ashdale was half across the
water, and after ten minutes or a quarter of an
hour she returned to shore, safe and sound. The
getting out was not so easy, but was accomplished
without even a wet foot.

"Do you think I can go, Captain Ashdale ? "
Violet was not courageous : she hated bulls and
thunderstorms ; but that's excusable. Must we
add that she preferred a carriage to riding,
excepting on a steady cob-like animal which was
more likely to tumble down than anything else in
the world? But Violet had an idea that she
should like to have a turn on the lake, and certainly quite as well with Frank Beauclerc as with
any one else. So she got in, not so cleverly as
Evelyn Ashdale; she was less of a sailor, or anything else, than that young lady, being younger,

and entirely under petticoat government: but she got in, after a little scream or two, and sat down. "Only sit still, Violet," said Frank Beauclerc.

The weather had changed a little. The day had been more than hot—sultry: and now there was a little wind rising. Lord Portarlington might have predicted a change within three days without risk of his reputation. Away went the wherry, and in two or three minutes Violet was reassured. They hailed the other boat, pulled alongside, changed greetings, but were prudent enough not to shake hands. The large party was a merry one: there was a charming little song sweetly enough sung by Mrs. Colville; Lady Clara never did such a thing without a piano. Colonel Twigg broke down in "Molly Carew," but Major Boldover came to the rescue with the "Low-backed Car;" so they pulled one way supremely happy, and Frank pulled the other, towards a pretty waterfall at the lower end of the lake, equally so.

The voyage had been accomplished in safety,

and they started to return. Frank had been on the water often enough to know that an inland lake is a treacherous sea, with any wind on. The too cautious mariner hugs the shore : but in this case his tactics were right. He pulled close under the trees which here clothed the water's edge. At one point he would have to leave this shelter and make for the landing-place across an open arm of the lake. It was but a couple of hundred yards more, and the comers were hailed with shouts of "Tea and the cottage." As he came from the shelter of the wooded bank, a sharp and sudden squall caught Violet's parasol : she always acted upon natural impulse, and that impulse was to save it. In one moment she was in the water, and, catching at the boat to save herself, the cranky outrigger careened over, filled, and went down.

Poor child ! The scream that was borne to the shore reached the ears of those who were already ascending the hill, while Frank, evading her attempts to get hold of him, caught her in a

powerful grasp, and began swimming with his
disengaged hand.   As fast as we write, a boat was
being unchained from her moorings : at least it
seemed so to him.

"Still, Violet, still, for the love of Heaven!
The boat's coming!   Violet, Violet, for God's
sake quiet, and we are safe !"   But Violet strug-
gled with that fear that is unequalled in this
world; the fear of death to the strong, the happy,
the young, the prosperous.   But the boat was not
coming, and the shouts of "Break the chain,"
"Here's the padlock," "The key, the key—who
has the key?" showed that all was not right.   At
last she fainted ; and then Frank felt his task
lighter; but he prayed mentally for help, as he
made but little way with his burthen.

At that moment a dark form, without coat or
hat, was seen to emerge from the shore, at the
nearest point, and with powerful strokes to swim
towards the exhausted pair.   Fresh and unem-
barrassed, it took him but a minute or two to
reach them, just as Frank was beginning to feel

his strength go. "Hold on, sir, one more stroke
or two, while I get the other side of her." At
that moment she slipped from Frank's grasp as
the new comer caught her beneath the arm, and
raised her face again above the surface. Favoured by the relief, and cheered by the manifest
capability of his friend, Frank made a few more
efforts, and, between them, they carried the inani-
mate form of poor Violet Carloss to the bank.

CHAPTER XI.

VIOLET'S TRUSTEES.

Avarice is a weed that will grow in a barren soil.

GREAT was the consternation among the
dowagers, and the sympathy among the young:
but neither of them would have brought back life
to those pallid cheeks but for other remedies.
An old woman, who had no sympathy, had a
flannel petticoat, hot as the day had been; and
the tea-kettle and blankets supplied other revivers.
The old soldier had nobly earned the reward
which was pressed upon him, and before he went
away only asked the name of the lady and gen-

tleman he had helped to rescue. " Miss Carloss!
He knew the family in India : and Mr. Beauclerc
too : he'd heard of him before :" and Frank gave
him his address, and told him the Colonel would
be glad to see him often, when he came home,
which he expected him to do some day, this year
or next.

" We owe you a couple of lives, my good
fellow : I couldn't have held on much longer,
and the boat never could have reached us in
time."

" Your honour, a big dog would a done it
better. Maybe I'll take cold : so I'll wish you
good evening, and the young lady too. I'll get
to Portbridge very well with the drop of drink
the gentlemen has given me."

So while they all ran backwards and forwards
in the cottage to wait upon Violet, the principal
actor disappeared from the scene. Modesty gives
great strength and beauty even to the absent, whilst
the vain we must have ever with us to be admired. Bacon says that it is as natural to die

as to be born: very likely; and a necessity
equally forced upon us.   It is strange the most
important personage has the least to say in
either matter.

Who that had seen Violet Carloss suspected
how near that bright, joyous, lifelike spirit was
to the cheerless grave.   For days she lay between life and death at the cottage of Madame
Rosenfels.   "The shock to her system had been
great," said our village Esculapius, with a profundity which alarmed us all.   We were none of
us good enough ourselves to endorse the pious sentiment of that very worthy, but rather Calvinistic,
Mrs. Betel Crusher to her friend Mrs. Manning.
"Would Providence be pleased to take her
before she became the miserable thing that she
must be, now while she was comparatively innocent?"   We did not think with these two ladies
upon that occasion, but prayed fervently that
He would restore her to us.   But then we had
not three daughters like Mrs. Crusher, who
sought husbands from amongst the eligible of

Lymmersfield. Doubtless there were plenty there who knew that nothing so natural, and so inevitable, as death could be designed as an evil; but we had our own selfish wishes upon the subject, and preferred that it should come at a natural time. Death in one so young, so healthful, so beautiful, we regarded as neither natural nor inevitable, but as an exceptional dispensation of Providence; and we prayed accordingly. Mesdames Crusher and Manning had taken a wrong view of the case this time, and in the course of a week or ten days Violet Carloss was herself again.

Excepting in the way of gratitude, poured out in torrents of words, which seemed to be carried down on the stream of her tears, she did not love to talk about her accident. She shut her eyes when it was casually mentioned, and most of her neighbours got to respect her fears. So in a few months it came to be forgotten. "Frank," she said, the day before he astonished Chelsea Hospital and its wooden-legged pensioners with his learning, " I shall never forget it, nor to thank you for it. Two days after, when they thought I might die, and told me how much better and happier I should be out of this world, I felt more than ever grateful to you for your brave struggles for me. Ah! if ever I see our poor soldier again, what shall I do for him? and you can't find his address. Ah! a life at sixteen is a great debt to owe : but I'm glad I have it, and that I owe it to you."

" But you are less my debtor than you think, Violet. Your brother never told you that he had done the same for me at Grammerton :" and then he tried to relieve her sense of obligation by an account of the battle of the punts in his school-boy days.

" Never mind, Frank, it makes no difference who saved your life : you saved mine, and I never knew how dear it was to me till that dreadful moment."

Here Violet tried to assume her usually defiant tone, but she was unsuccessful. She put her hands up to shut out the painful vision, and the tears trickled slowly through her fingers. Frank got up from his seat, and, as she held out a hand to him to say good-bye, he stooped down and kissed her forehead. He did not wait to see its effect, but walked quickly out of the room.

Then came the business of the examination.

Bentley, and Standish, and Frank Beauclerc represented the strength of the Lymmersfield stable. They sat down outside the hall at Chelsea to compare notes under the long porticos. "Let's look at your Euclid paper, Standish:" and that youth produced a rough draught of what he had sent up to Mr. Heavyside. He had proved beyond all question than two sides of a triangle were greater than the third, but he had also given his opinion at the end of the proof that "that was absurd." Professor Heavyside not agreeing with that view, nor indeed with some others, as to the value of certain rectangles and squares, or the mode of competing heights and distances adopted by this gentleman, forgot to put his name down in the list which was afterwards presented to the British public through the valuable columns . of the *Times* newspaper. As Bentley had confidently stated that William Rufus was Charles the First's nephew, and that he had lost the battle of Marston Moor by his rashness, it is not wonderful that his knowledge of English history was called in question by Professor Chepmell. He had written, it is true, an elaborate essay on Roman Law and Agrarian Outrage, which ought to have given him the command of a squadron at least, but the English failure was too palpable, besides which he wrote "Triggernometry" as if it had something to do with sport.

Frank sat on the benches outside, too, and compared notes with the rest. He was not strong in French, which had a decidedly Grammertonian twang. The Welsh gentleman had been manifestly employed.

" What did you put for these derivations, Beauclerc ? "

" Well, they rather floored me," said Frank, " to tell you the truth."

"So they did me," said Standish, evidently astonished that he should have been floored by anything, after such a careful preparation from the modern school. "What did you say 'grouse' was derived from?"

"Nothing at all," said Beauclerc; "you didn't think they meant γρυς (grus), because that's a crane; and that's not much like a grouse, you know. What did you put for that?"

"Well, I was regularly floored, too; would you believe it?"

"Certainly, if you say so."

Standish was not good at a joke, so he continued, "But the fellow next to me was a regular clever fellow: did everything, and no mistake. And, do you know, he shoved his paper over to me just at that very question, and pointed to that word; and then I saw 'grouse,' a Moorish word; so I copied it, of course."

Here Frank went into a fit of laughter, and even Bentley, not remarkable for a sense of humour, followed his example. "And I hope you thanked your neighbour for his valuable assistance ? "

" Yes, I did afterwards, and he seemed to be rather annoyed."

" Why, what did he say ? "

" Well, he wasn't very polite. He said, ' What a confounded idiot you must be ; we shall both be shut out for copying. It's only a joke.' "

And so out of the three Colville had two of them back again ; and their fathers hoped they worked hard, and that Mr. Colville would keep their noses to the grindstone. At the same time, these judicious parents sent them back with a very liberal supply of money, and a very moderate supply of advice ; the main article of the latter being not to smoke too much. They also regretted that their boys had not read much during the vacation, as they had been obliged to give them some indulgence in Scotland after their hard work in the previous half-year.

One morning not long after these events (it was in October), Madame Rosenfels and the Rev. Harry Colville sat opposite to one another in the charming little room which Madame devoted to her own studies in "The Cottage," as it was called, at Lymmersfield. She looked much as usual; earnest, however, and clever, and remarkably well. There was a great deal of intellect in her face, but of not a very high character. It was not the intelligence of refinement or cultivation. She was not above small fascinations, to which truly great or good women rarely condescend. She twisted her rings, which were numerous and handsome, and the clear veins showed in a long and somewhat nervous hand, which was of a sufficiently good colour. Her foot *bien chaussé* was very busy, and hung out its peculiar lure. Those well-shod women have it sometimes *bien forchu.* Altogether there was so much to fascinate that a good physiognomist would have been on his guard. Harry Colville was not versed in the wiles of the female boa constrictor.

He was a very different person from his hostess. He was plain enough. Some people wondered how Bessie Frampton could have married so plain a person, "and without a shilling too, my dear."

Bessie Frampton liked a companion, not a dummy; hence it came that she pleased herself in the matter. Of dummies, young ladies, one is quite as good as another, so take the one with the most gilt on it. Harry Colville, however, had his ornamental side, if you turned him round. He was a perfect gentleman, always well dressed, cleanly and fresh-looking, and delighting in those inestimable advantages, hands and feet. If you have them not, don't try to make them; that always fails. Adopt the present " high-low" or " shooting-boot" fashion, and go about without gloves. Where there is no pretension, much will not be expected. Colville was a clever man, too; acute, and with an intellect of a much higher order than that of Madame. He never descended to cunning. He had plenty of tact, too, and a manner acquired in the best society, from which his professional duties only debarred him during nine months of the year. There was one thing, however, of which he knew nothing; that universal acquaintance with affairs, one's own or other people's, which goes by the name of

" business." He was no match for Madame in this matter.

" Then, if I understand you rightly, you think the money would be more profitably invested in this building land than it is now; and that it would add to Violet's comfort and your own."

" Oh! my dear Mr. Colville," and she laid that very clever-looking but tenacious hand upon his arm (I don't like it myself, I confess, when I intend to oppose a lady's proposition), my dear Mr. Colville, for myself I have enough, and am well satisfied; but for Violet, both now and hereafter it would be a great advantage to have six or seven per cent. instead of three, which she is getting now." She forgot to say anything of the security of the Funds; Colville knew as much about it as he did about the exchange between Cairo and London. Investing money had never been one of his amusements.

" Certainly, there can be no doubt about it, Madame. It's very thoughtful of you; and I suppose you have seen Shearham about it, for you know it's not much in my way. Perhaps you don't mind explaining which land it is you think of buying?"

"You know, Mr. Colville, that the value of property has increased very much here."

"I believe so;" and Colville then thought about an article he was writing for the *Temple Bar*.

"And is still increasing," added the lady with some pertinacity.

"No doubt of it. I should think Lymmersfield, from what I hear, is likely to be overrun with bricks and mortar."

"And that increases the value of property so much," said Madame again.

"It won't increase the value of mine, I'm afraid."

"Well, perhaps not, if you don't wish to sell. But I hope you have no idea of leaving Lymmersfield. If you have, it will. You know the Squire has sold the whole of the property excepting the Hall and the Park, which is to go when the Barringtons' lease is out."

" I've heard so; and I'm sorry for it. So pretty
a place near London ought not to be cut to pieces.
It's the only real country suburb left."

" Then I am afraid you won't like my project. I
should like to invest for Violet in some of that
land for building purposes. There could be no
risk, and the advantage to dear Violet would be
very great. But of course, if you don't wish
it——" Madame put on an injured face, and
played with her wedding-ring; and was Colville
the man to raise imaginary objections? " She'll
really be a rich person in ten years' time, if she
sells out a few hundreds now."

" And what you want is my consent, I presume?"
rejoined he, hesitatingly.

" Well, I—that is—Major Carloss's wishes were
that you should be always consulted, and, you
know, I wouldn't act without doing what I believed to be right: so that I am glad to think you
do not disapprove." An assumption."

" No, oh, no! of course not: anything that is
desirable for Violet, why—naturally—only see

Shearham, and get the thing put straight. So
you really think that Lymmersfield property is
likely to increase in value, Madame?"

" I'm very glad I've a long lease of the cottage."

"And I'm very glad I bought my place when
I had the opportunity. And where are you going
this autumn?" he was glad to escape further
money matters.

" Well! I shall be off to Brighton," said Madame, whose spirits had wonderfully recovered
themselves at the success of her negotiation. "The
leaves are all about, and this place is a little damp
at the fall of the year. You may judge of the increase of property here: I've let my cottage for
the winter—mind, the winter—for six guineas a
week." Confirmation strong, thought he: so he
said:

" Have you really? And when do you go?"

" Next week—but we shall come to say good-
by—and I hope Mrs. Colville or Alice may be per-
suaded to come and stay with us, while you go for
your six weeks' hunting to Lord Wodecraft's."

" That's very kind of you indeed, Madame. I know they would like it very much: but your friend, the Griffin, has been a great absentee lately. I've nobody to cut the newspaper or butter my toast when she's away. I thought of borrowing Violet."

" I hope Mr. Beauclerc is well? " Madame now was anxious to change the subject.

" Very, when I heard. He expects his father in England next year. My love to Violet, Madame." And Colville took leave, with his mind wondering what he should do with the New Zealanders, whom he was endeavouring to put straight before the world in the pages of *Temple Bar*.

What Madame Rosenfels had said of Lymmersfield was true. It was being shamefully built over, and the value of property was increasing proportionately as its beauty decreased. Her present object was to do as she had done before: to buy with Violet's money, and sell as the market got better, putting the difference into her own pocket. She had done so before, and found it profitable : I suppose she had no idea, as a trustee, that it was illegal. When, however, people meddle with bricks and mortar, they never know where to stop. Of one thing she was quite clear, at all events ; that Violet was a valuable possession, and Madame made up her mind that the longer she could keep her the better. It required no great intelligence to see that.

" There is safety in numbers," said she, as she carried her off to Brighton in the beginning of the fashionable season. "Anywhere out of easy reach of Portbridge."

Colville returned home from his visit to touch up the New Zealanders, and to pursue that ingenious process of making silk purses out of swine's ears. Having never formally undertaken to act as a trustee with Madame, and having entrusted the active exercise of the duty to herself and Mr. Shearham, he enjoyed a part of the moral responsibility with some of the pleasures of interference. His position in this respect was altogether anomalous. Madame Rosenfels herself had almost begun to regard his counsel as an impertinence: but, like many persons of mixed character, she was unwilling to discard the mask of respectability which attached to apparent honesty of purpose, so long as her designs were not openly thwarted. The lady, it will be seen, was essentially that which the gentleman was not—a woman of business, of action, of deliberate determination: and when years before the old Eastbourne physician had offered a craniological opinion on her character, he had been singularly appreciative of her talents. Colville was a clever man: far cleverer as a man than Madame was as a woman: but he was deficient in energy, unless pitted against men, upon subjects which interested him. Hence his almost unintelligible acceptance of a position, which Madame Rosenfels had made for him: that of sleeping partner in a very bad business. The redeeming part in it was one which he never considered; his legal freedom from responsibility. It was well for Madame that Mrs. Colville had not the management of these affairs.

CHAPTER XII.

OUR VILLAGE.

Variety's the source of joy below.—GAY.

LYMMERSFIELD had its parties, and very strong ones they were—social, religious, and political. It was the business of Harry Colville and his wife to know everybody: so they did: not intimately, but as a gentleman who occasionally did the duty in the parish church, with a kind and neighbourly feeling; which is better far than a familiarity, which frequently breeds contempt.

Dufferling, the chairman of the Puffanblow Railway Company, and a great man in the City, but whose fame had never reached Lymmersfield till he came to live there, was a leader of one party. He lived in a large white house, had a great lady in many senses for a wife, and a numerous family which appeared to be all feathers, black velvet, and scarlet stocking, with plenty of hair. His want of liberality impaired somewhat his popularity. He took a large part in everything which cost him nothing, and acted on a grand principle of getting all he could out of everybody. He was an imposing-looking person, with plenty of whisker, an intelligent baldness, and great severity of white waistcoat. He had much heartiness of manner, and tendered his advice and indeed assistance at times. He parted freely enough with everything but money. "Pay the fellow liberally, and let him go," said he, always in reference to somebody else's expenses; or, "I should be delighted to subscribe, or do anything I could for the poor fellow, but it's impossible to break through a principle." His charity began at home, and stopped there.

Plantagenet Twigg was one of his followers. He called himself a general merchant, a City man, being indeed a simple and prosperous maltster, and to be seen any day in a crowded thoroughfare near Leadenhall-street. There he indulged in mighty speculations: sugars by the hogshead, cigars by the hundred-weight, tallow by the cask, and French wines by the brand : anything, in fact, but malt. He had plenty of money, was a great patron of Poole and Bartley, an authority on hunting on a small scale; was a generous, good-natured, unrefined specimen of British industry, and liked to dine at the great white house occasionally, where he was allowed to meet the élite of the village. Privately he has been heard to declare that Dufferling was a screw, to which he prefixed a weighty expletive.

There were half a dozen more of the same sort who shared the same extensive hospitality. They all kept broughams, and sympathised in a common jealousy of Barrington. "Who the deuce was Barrington, they should like to know; to give himself airs: just because he had married an Earl's daughter?"

Then there were the jovial, devil-may-care barristers, some with briefs, and some without: all free and easy, laugh-compelling gentlemen with plenty of whisker, but cleanly shorn chins. They smoked together, and had their own jokes, and dined in town, coming down by the late train, who wouldn't have Dufferling at any price. Indeed they much preferred Twigg, who had not much to say about literature and the *Saturday Review*, but opened his cigar-case to them as they went up to chambers every morning. They dined so well at their clubs and in town, that they didn't care for the fish and soup, and the badly cooked entrées, and the joint, and the splendid plate which they got down at Lymmersfield; but knocked up a chop dinner among themselves, and discussed Gladstone's "Homer," and the Chancellor's Law Reforms, and light French literature, and the Rotten Row beauties, and the demi-monde in general. They were a little irregular at church,

and cut splendid jokes on the mercantile broughams and their occupants.

There was a strong religious party headed by
Mr. Manning. He carried away the old women
and the unappropriated females, the curate, and
the respectable well-to-do gossips of the place.
They did much good too in their way. They
headed subscription lists with gigantic liberality
that astonished the Dufferling party, from whom
they demanded money, not principles. Their wives,
assisted by Mrs. Colville, did the Dorcas and
flannel-petticoat societies, and looked after the poor
women, who were said to be one too many for an
unmarried curate. They were good praiseworthy
people, and had their reward in the conscious rectitude of their own intentions and the ceaseless
ingratitude of their opponents. There is nothing
people hate so much as being reminded of their
duties; so, they christened the worthy lawyer
the Solicitor-General.

Lymmersfield had, too, its gossiping shops. None
equalled the morning train to London-bridge.

" How are you, Dufferling ? So Barrington has lost a lot of money, I hear, by the Liverpool Steeple-chase ?" So spoke Plantagenet Twigg, who was bound to be posted in sport.

" I did hear something about it," says the chairman, exposing his breast to the morning breeze, for it was not the right thing to be behindhand in intelligence.

" Indeed ? I hear he's likely to go," added Rumford, of the War Office.

" Sad thing for Lady Clara : his horses are going to Tattersall's next week." This was partly true, as a detachment of screws was going to be disposed of preparatory to a fresh instalment. " As to Barrington, I always did think him a great fool. Thinks a monstrous deal of himself."

" Not so bad a fellow when you know him," said young Potts, the distiller, who had a slight bowing acquaintance with him, engendered from the sale of a barren Alderney, in which Barrington's bailiff had got so much the best of the bargain, that his master's heart was softened, and he offered to take her back.

"Very extraordinary thing about Manning," said Plantagenet.

"What's the matter now?" inquired his neighbour.

"He guaranteed the money for the repairs of the church; and he's nearly fifty pounds short. They've sued him, and he'll have to pay."

"What's he going to do?" says Potts: "he can afford it, I suppose."

"He's going to have a subscription, and a sermon, and that sort of thing, you know."

"That I shall set my face against, on principle," says the Chairman of the Puffanblow Railway. "I refused to subscribe at first, and it would be impossible to give way now." Here he involuntarily buttoned his pocket.

"But he don't want you to give way, Mr. Chairman; he wants you to give money," said Potts.

"By Jove!" says Leader. "Come in here, Slasher; how are you? What do you think Blathewicke says of the service, since the choir has been established?"

"No idea what the learned Serjeant may have perpetrated: nothing too bad for him."

"Why! Young Banks, the carpenter, leads the choir: so he calls him Banks and Brays."

"My dear Mrs. Meddell, I assure you that's the fact. Violet Carloss, poor girl, is quite off her head: and Madame Rosenfels is gone to consult Dr. Sutherland." Thus spoke our old acquaintance, Mrs. Betel Crusher.

"Ah! that comes of their pic-nics and water parties: I said so, all along. What could they expect? And what's become of Mr. Beauclerc? I recollect him so high." Here the lady put out a small umbrella. "I'm sure I always gave him credit for being a very steady young man."

"Oh! I don't blame him so much, I'm sure. But there's Mr. Colville, he knows no more of the world than a baby: just see how they've brought up their own daughter, going all over the country by herself, and painting signs, and I don't know what. And that Madame, as they call her. Ah! I've no patience with your Madames, indeed;" and here Mrs. Boxer, the widow of the late respected Boxer, F.C.S. and M.D., of Lymmersfield, indulged in sundry nods and winks to her neighbours, and sighed deeply.

Mrs. Boxer was one of the kindest-hearted women alive, and would have taken Violet Carloss to her bosom at a moment's notice; but the atmosphere of the train was redolent of scandal, and she couldn't resist.

In the mean time, Violet and Madame were enjoying themselves exceedingly by the seaside.

The trade of the place, too, was an euphemism for robbery: two hundred per cent. on all goods; and good behaviour and prompt payment required to get what you wanted at all. Lymmersfield was a close borough, and lacked contesting.

Lymmersfield stood on a hill; and at the top of the hill was a grand public. Its proprietor called it the hotel, as indeed it had been long time ago, when at least fifty coaches changed horses in the village, and as many pairs of posters were wanted

to convey the aristocracy down the Portbridge
road. But the mighty were fallen. It provided
three horses and two flys, and, having a cantan-
kerous sort of landlord, was altogether at a discount. It was nearly unfrequented.

Its great institution was the tap ; and here the
butcher's son, the young corn-chandler (a great
authority on the doings of the Ring, and an uncom-
promising studier of the *Sporting Life*), young
joiners engaged on job, and the local vet., with their
associates, met every evening for the discussion of
village news. Nor was it always confined to these.
It would have been a gratifying sight to Pater-
familias who encourages smoking at home, as a
harmless amusement, or winks at it as a necessary
evil, to have looked in upon the company at odd
times, on which the student-life of England re-
cruited exhausted nature.

" How did you get out, Standish ?" said Bentley,
who wore a billycock hat very much on one side,
and a short-waisted duckhunter, with a small cane
in one pocket.

" Colville thinks I'm in the garden." Colville

did not, and was only waiting an opportunity to tell that gentleman that he should decline giving him a testimonial to the Horse Guards, unless he was more particular in the company he kept. " I got over the wall, and I shall go back the same way," added he.

" Hallo! Gorschampton; how did you get here?"

" I had leave to go up to town," said his Lordship; " and I've never been home."

" Well, then, stop and have a pipe," said Pitt, who had just joined them.

" No: I promised to be home at eight, and it's very near that now." His Lordship had some regard for his word. " Hallo! what's this? Beauclerc gazetted to the —— Hussars. Has any fellow heard from him?"

" Yes," said Pitt, " I have: I'm going to Maidstone on Saturday to dine and sleep: he says he's very jolly. Did you expect him to get through so high, Bentley?"

" No. I knew he was safe enough—at least,

Colville said so, but five thousand and one takes a deal of getting. I wonder where the one comes from?"

"It must be a curiously close computation—one fellow got through by one run, one mark, I mean —closish shaving. Eighteen hundred and one."

"Better than no shaving at all," said Pitt. This was rather an inconsiderate remark of Mr. Pitt's, seeing that it was addressed to an unsuccessful competitor. "Isn't Beauclerc coming here to see us, or is he too great a swell now?"

"I wonder he hasn't been to see Violet Carloss since he got through."

"If he's going to Maidstone, he won't think much more about Lymmersfield. Jolly place Maidstone is, I can tell you. My brother was quartered there for I don't know how long. Lots of fun, visiting, and dining, and hunting, and dancing, and all that."

"So I should think," said Gorsehampton. "We've all heard of the Kentish hops." As no one had ever heard of the produce of that county,

the joke would have fallen quite flat, but for the
arrival of the butcher's boy, who heard it in the
midst of the enjoyment of a glass of ale which he
had called for.   He burst out laughing, dispersing
his beer pretty freely over the floor; and wiping
his mouth with the back of his sleeve, he said:

"Danged if that ain't good now, Bentley; I call
that first chop, I do."

"Well, that's a subject you ought to know something about," replied Bentley, looking very sulky
at the freedom of his young associate.

"Who the devil's that?" said his Lordship,
rather astonished that a stranger should have taken
the liberty of applauding a joke of his.

"Oh! it's only that fool, Suet: he's always here
making a row."

"Is he?" said the young Earl, taking up his
hat and walking straight out of the room.   It was
his first visit to the taproom of the Fox and
Hounds, and he took care that it was the last.

"That's a blackguard place," said his Lordship,
when his companions returned home, very unfit

for the historical lecture which they professed to attend in the study from nine to ten. "That's a blackguard place, and, if I were you fellows, I wouldn't go any more. I know Colville hates it, and wouldn't stand it if he was to catch us. It's all very well smoking a pipe and having a glass of beer, but I can't stand young Suet and Macgrane, with his long jaw about Nobby Hall and the Nigger. I wouldn't go there any more, if I were you fellows, dashed if I would." And as his opinion was worth something, the tap for a time went out of fashion, and the village festivities were not enlivened by the presence of the sons of two Masters of Fox-hounds, of a Member of Parliament, and the nephew of a Cabinet Minister.

Distinguishing justly between village life and low life, and having no taste for the latter, I shall decline entering upon its characteristics any further, as exhibited by the mixed company of the Fox and Hounds of Lymmersfield. Frank Beauclerc had other ideas of pleasure and of duty, and without

being a model pupil, was satisfied with the position
and society which education and accident had en-
tailed upon him. I do not think his industry was
equal to the structure of a great name or a large
fortune: but there was a consistency about him,
joined to an elasticity of intellect, which would
have kept him from falling below his level. Of one
thing you might be quite certain, that he never
would have risen by unworthy means. Nature
had made him a gentleman, and education had
completed the work by making him a Christian.
The practical result of birth and training in Lord
Gorsehampton was the same; but with a difference.
As long as the circumstances of the case were easy
and ordinary, practically the two men would have
stood on equal ground in the eyes of the world.
In strong temptation the latter might have failed;
the former would have assuredly conquered. There
was something to back a sense of high truth in
Frank, which would give him unflinching determination in difficulties, and a superiority to defeat.
How many fathers send their sons to Eton or

Harrow to become gentlemen? I wonder at their notion of the word. A few, who would have been such without it, strengthen their position by tact and worldly knowledge, good manners, and facile scholarship. A vast majority mistake fast living for *savoir faire*, and low life for independence of character.

But Frank Beauclerc was gone, and his mantle had fallen on Lord Gorsehampton's shoulders. He had a host of Ahabs to practise upon.

"I say, Gorsehampton, Beauclerc's gazetted to the —— Hussars."

"How do you know? Have you had a letter?" said his Lordship.

"No: I saw it in the paper, up at the Fox." [N.B.—This was the short for the sign of the aforesaid public-house.]

"Where's the regiment?"

"At Maidstone. He got through rather well."

"Do you know why? because, if not, I'll tell you." It will be perceived that this young aristocrat was tolerably free spoken. "Because he preferred reading at home to smoking and drinking at the village public : and if you're wise, Pitt, you'll do the same."

Pitt reflected : and reflection is very valuable and very rare at his time of life. We haven't much to do with him or his companions when Frank is once launched into life, but we may as well say that he was just one of that numerous class who, being but slightly impressed by precept, has the more to learn from example. "I can't understand the pleasures of talking to young Suet and Macgrane, with his eternal nonsense about the 'hodds' on this ''orse,' and the 'hodds' on the other. He never puts the 'hodds' on the proper shoulders. If I were you fellows, I wouldn't go there any more."

The young delinquents were more successful at their next examination.

CHAPTER XIII.

JUST JOINED.

We are but warriors for a working day.
                                    SHAKESPEARE.

In times of peace the lives of young cavalry officers do not differ much from one another. A little duty, which our colonels expect to have well done; a good mess; a general welcome in the county, which is of course due to their moral and intellectual superiority over any other branch of the service; an unquestioned right to a moustache, which of late years has been shared with Government clerks, ambitious curates, all the Infantry, and most of the Volunteers, make life pleasant as

well as ornamental. The dress is becoming, and
particularly useful in a ball-room, where it is calculated to keep off intruders in a crowd, and to
make great employment for the underpaid and
overworked milliners' girls—a debt to that class of
the fair sex which is fairly due from gentlemen
who are said to have such eminent success among
them. The hunting-field is recommended, indeed
insisted upon, by the press, as the one great school for
cavalry officers : and France is at all times pointed
to as an illustrious example of its infallibility.
Character is developed by the matutinal and post-
prandial cigar ; a judgment for claret is cultivated ;
steeple-chasing gives a tone to the stomach for the
steward's ordinary, and a dignified contempt for
cold water in cold blood ; while not only a taste
for, but a quickness in, calculation is attained by
constant attendance on the race-course, and an
unchecked confidence in laying or taking the odds.
These are a few of the *agrémens* which assume the
position of duties in a crack cavalry corps ; and
Frank Beauclerc was not slow to profit by them.

But we must do Frank justice. He was no coward, but he was not a man to take a header without first ascertaining the depth of the water and his own capability for swimming. Neither had he that obliquity of moral vision which pretends to see virtue in vice, because it comes with a gilded exterior. He knew the real value of most things, seen even through the refracted rays of pleasure and enthusiasm. He became a great favourite in his regiment : in fact, the most popular man that had joined since poor Flatman, who was killed in a run from Balleycasey Castle. To be sure, there's a great deal of ill-directed ardour in popularity. The British public, or the officers of a regiment, follow a cry as staunchly as a pack of hounds score to the cry of one leader, and sometimes have to be whipped off hare. It is very fickle too, and somewhat vulgar. There is a glare, and a heat, and a crowd about the movements of a popular man, which either oppress and restrain him in following the bent of his own tastes, or urge him to an unnatural anticipation of the tastes of his pursuers. In fact, like the fox, who is taking the lead for safety and to avoid the pressure of the crowd behind, he seems to be playing the same game; when, all the time, he is conscious of a danger which is being forced upon him, hazardously and unfortunately. Popular men should be leniently criticised : they are not their own masters. Like drunkards, they are acting under a pressure of circumstances; but, unlike them, they are not even responsible for the cause. Only one out of a thousand is allowed to lead from beginning to end. Poor Flatman ! He spent all his money in the cause, all his time, and a great deal of his health, and killed himself in support of the prestige of the —— Hussars with the Balleycasey Hounds. The unpopular man who applauds himself at home is at least as fortunate as this.

Frank's popularity, however, was not of this kind : it was of a better class altogether. By the time he had left the depôt and had been with his regiment a twelvemonth or more, he had acquired a character, as well as a popularity, which did as

much good to others as to himself. He was more
like the leading hound than the fox : and he gave
a good healthy tone to the regimental subalterns,
which acted indirectly upon those who were of
longer service and higher grade.

"That's a promising young officer, Major, that
Frank Beauclerc. I don't know when we've had
such a good-looking, active youngster join us.
Certainly not since I've had the regiment."

"Indeed he is, Colonel," said Major Steadiman,
a Scotch gentleman who had gained his present
position from the ranks by transcendent courage
and an undeviating course of honourable duty, not
without a necessary economy for which his coun-
trymen are considered famous. "Indeed he is, a
vara extra-a-ordinary young mon : a leetle inclined
to be gay, to be sure——"

"Come, Major, I think you're a leetle inclined
to be hypercritical," said the Colonel.

The Major did not quite understand what that
was, but proceeded to defend his position.

"Na doubt, Colonel, the callant's as fine a

looking soldier-like mon as ever put foot into stir-
rup ; but he's ower fond of hunting his chargers ;
and I'm told — mind, I don't speak of my own
knowledge—that both his hacks can race."

"Well, it's difficult for a youngster, with
money, to live in a regiment like this without
some taste for horseflesh : it's part of his profession,
Major ; besides, he's no gambler even in that; he
never puts on above a tenner, and that with a
brother-officer.   We were young ourselves once."

The Colonel asserted this with an eye to a
moral juvenility, in which, it should be remarked,
the Major had never had any part.   "I'm no
speaking against the young mon, Colonel; he's
the smartest officer and the best rider we have in
the corps, and he's the vara quickest and steadiest
coachman I ever sat behind : but I'm no friend
to the Turf, Colonel."

"Nor I, Major; I've seen too much of it.
Men do begin, as you say, with their tenners " (not
that the Major had said so, for he would have
called it a " ten-pund note"), " and go on, like

bricks and mortar, till they never know where to stop. But I don't think Frank Beauclerc is likely to commit himself in that way."

"Maybe not: but it's ill playing wi' edged tools. There's no gentleman of my acqueentance that has raised himself by assorting wi' bad company; and a great many that have brought mickle grief to themselves and their families."

"I'm told he's a capital billiard-player. That's a more dangerous accomplishment than the other, to my mind," said the Colonel.

"I never see a young gentleman knocking about the balls, as they call it, in a public room, without thinking him a fool, and premising that he will become a knave, if Providence has only given him brains for the situation."

"Frank Beauclerc doesn't want them, at all events: let's hope he may use them to another purpose, Major. Here's his health." And the jolly Colonel drained a glass of sherry and pushed the bottle to his companion. "One more glass."

"I remember his father weel in India. He

was as like him as twa peas; but younger-looking and not so steady. He'd one great fault, Colonel. He never said 'no.' He was a mighty favourite with us all. Everybody loved him; and when he married, there wasn't a woman out there that wasn't ready to break her heart."

"I've heard he was not very happy in his choice," said Colonel Hoplight.

"I never heard that he replaced the first Mrs. Beauclerc wi' a second, and it's no gude sign that, Colonel."

"No, but there was some curious story about him and some lady up in the country."

"Yes, there was: when he was up in the hills —but that was after his wife's death some length of time—and nobody ever knew the rights o' the story. The ladies in Calcutta—that's them he didn't pay much attention to—were vara wroth for a time; but when he came back they received him wi' all the honours. Ye see then he was a widower, and his uncle had died in the

mean time. He opened a great ball at Calcutta wi' the Judge-Advocate's lady, and that
put the whole matter right: but I hear he didn't
marry Sir Joseph Parchment's daughter after
all."

The stalwart Major here rose, and, wishing the
Colonel a good evening, retired to his quarters;
while the Colonel himself, lighting a cigar, after
exchanging his coat for a smoking-jacket, proceeded to look over his book on the Grand
Military, in which his pet cornet and one of
his captains were engaged. As he appreciated
Frank's forbearance in the betting-ring, we hope
he found his account satisfactory, and not too
heavy.

"Hallo! Beauclerc, what are you going to do
to-morrow?" said the junior lieutenant.

"Nothing at all," said Frank, meaning that he
had no particular engagement that need prevent
him from joining any agreeable amusement proposed to him.

"Then, by Jove! old fellow, I wish you'd take
my duty: I want to go to Leamington; and we're

ordered to Brighton next week : I shan't have another chance."

" Ordered to Brighton : what's that for ? "

" To relieve the Fifteenth. Capital quarters : lots of balls; and the season's just at its height. All the Jews and Jewesses gone last month, and the swells coming in." The speaker was Lieutenant the Honourable Tom Dashwood—a fair, tall, decidedly languid youth, with unexceptionable hands and feet, and a very delicately-formed nose. Just the thing for Leamington, where he made the *trottoir* to resound with his boots, and the clubs with his brilliant conversation. Tom Dashwood was a great lady-killer : indeed, time and women were his great victims, so that Brighton suited him to a turn. Nobody knew how Tom got rid of his money, but he was always dreadfully hard up.

" The Jews and Jewesses gone ? " replied Beauclerc—" that's a bad look out for you : you could kill two birds with one stone, Tom. What a thing it would be to put up at the Three Balls : what would Lord Tremencourt say ? "

"Oh! you're always chaffing a fellow. Will you take my duty to-morrow?"

"I believe you're after no good, Dashwood; tell us all about it. There's a woman at the bottom of it," said Frank, laughing. "Who is it?"

"Ah! I'm not going to tell you, old fellow; you'll be going over yourself. Will you take my turn to-morrow? Come, tell me that."

"Well, I will if you'll tell me her name," said Frank, still laughing; when in came Charlie Ryder. He had joined but a short time, and had already exhibited symptoms of pace which, whether in the field or elsewhere, is sure to end in grief. Charlie had all the characteristics of a spoilt child. He had blue eyes, long eyelashes, curly air, a good nose, slightly retroussé, laughing mouth, and a neat figure: was about five feet six, and a general professor. In fact, he was bidding fair for the popularity which Flatman had enjoyed, and which Beauclerc despised: and he really would have stood a good chance had he been only four inches taller. We forgot to say that it was after

luncheon, and that the mess-room was deserted;
so Charlie warmed himself in a gentlemanly manner, while the winter's sun stole in a quiet sickly
way in at the windows of the dull, ill-furnished
apartment.   It lighted up a portrait of General
Sir John Moore at Corunna.

"Who is it you're talking about, Beauclerc:
the woman at Leamington? Ah! isn't she a
stunner, that's all! She can give Miss Moss a
stone and a half, and walk in."

"You're improving, Charlie," said Lieutenant
Dashwood; while Frank looked at the two in
silence, and wondered whether her Majesty had
not a hard bargain in both of them.

"Ah! you're not much of a Leamington
man, Beauclerc: but I can tell you that Violet
Carloss isn't to be sneezed at.   Forty thousand
down, and such a stepper; isn't she, Dashwood?"

It would be difficult to say which blushed the
deeper: Beauclerc or Dashwood. Charlie Ryder
then began a catalogue raisonnée of her charms,
which Beauclerc thought right to interrupt by in-

forming them of his previous acquaintance with her. Not very long afterwards they separated, and as Frank went towards the stables he began to reflect upon the name of the girl whom he had scarcely seen since he joined, but whose image had been rarely absent from his thoughts.

Beauclerc had been but seldom to Lymmersfield. Without any intention of appearing indifferent, he acknowledged to himself that his visits to his old tutor had not been as frequent as they ought to have been. The visit or two that he had paid had been short and unsatisfactory, and on each occasion Violet and Madame had been absent the greater part of the time. He was not vain, or he might have wondered that they should have sought so little to improve his auspiciously begun acquaintance. Violet Carloss, he thought, was not likely to become enamoured of the *petits soins* of Tom Dashwood; but he felt a strong inclination to see for himself. As to Charlie Ryder, he, at all events, was completely out of the hunt. It was astonishing, however, how little he felt disposed to

gather information from either the one or the
other.

Violet Carloss had thought of Frank as a girl of
her temperament was likely to think of the man to
whom she owed so lasting an obligation. Madame
Rosenfels, it is true, had done her utmost to efface
the impression. She talked but little of him herself, and avoided the Colvilles as far as she could
do so. She was rather afraid of Mrs. Colville's
honesty, and having got Colville's signature to the
completion of her purchase, was not particularly
anxious for closer inquiries into the success of her
speculation. It had not turned out well as yet; and
the building mania was less rife than it had been.
Mr. Alderman Smithers, the wholesale purchaser,
had informed Mr. Shearham that he was not prepared to take any more lots at three hundred
pounds an acre. Madame Rosenfels had burnt
her fingers.

She seemed restless, too, and not so careful of her
ward's matrimonial interests as she should have
been. She eschewed eligible *partis;* and when the

Honourable Tom Dashwood demonstrated beyond a doubt his admiration for Violet, she determined upon beating a retreat from the Spa.

Three days later, Frank Beauclerc found that his horse, whose turn it was to go to Mitford Wood, wanted rest. He wanted none himself, so he made his way to Leamington. Not having ventured upon any inquiries from Tom Dashwood or Charlie Ryder, he turned himself over to the intelligence of the postmaster.

"Do you know the address of a lady of the name of Rosenfels?"

The master referred to his memoranda, and informed him that she was staying at 104, The Parade. So Frank sought the Parade, and found a very handsome jeweller's shop. Having knocked at the private door, he was answered by a slipshod maid, not by any means belonging to Madame Rosenfels's establishment.

"Is Madame Rosenfels staying here?" said Frank, looking at a deserted staircase with the carpets up.

" Please, sir, she and the young lady went away the day before yesterday."

" And where are their letters to be sent to: have they left no address?" Frank was rather surprised at the quickness of the move, as Tom Dashwood was in utter ignorance of any such intention.

" They talked about going somewhere to the seaside; but I'll go and ask, sir, if you'll step in a minute." Frank stepped in a minute, while the girl was heard in colloquy with Mrs. Furnival, whom she addressed by name, in the lower regions. "Please, sir, this is the card as she left with missus." Frank took it, and read in Violet's handwriting, "The Cottage, Lymmersfield."

" Then they're gone home!" said he to himself. It was astonishing how annoyed he was; and how the girl's image haunted him. Surely, he could not be in love. I don't think he put the question to himself in so homely a way as that.

He was walking down the Parade when he met with an old acquaintance coming up. A quick and a good-looking horse was always an attraction to Frank ; so while staring at the mud-bespattered rider, he heard himself addressed by name, and recognised his friend Bentley.

Bentley assured him that they had had a first-rate thing, and that Ryder of "his" had gone splendidly. We killed only three miles from here, and he's waiting for the train now, to put his horse on."

" Confound the fellow," thought Frank ; " now he'll tell that ass Dashwood that I've been here all day."

" What are you going to do, Beauclerc ? "

" I was on my way to the train."

" Oh ! never mind about Ryder. Come home and dine with me."

" I can't dress ; I've no clothes."

" Never mind about that. There's nobody coming but Fairfax."

" What time can I get away ? I must be in barracks to-night."

" There's a late train at ten thirty to Coventry. That will do for you. When I've left my horse, we'll go to the club for an hour or two, and we can dine at half-past six. Fairfax is sure to be there, and we'll tell him of the alteration."

Fairfax was there, and they told him of the alteration.

All young men seem to have a taste for what is called a little dinner; a potage, sole au gratin, or truites au capres (when you can get them), salmi de perdrix, canard aux olives, chapon, écrévisses, with some trifle of cabinet pudding, and crême à la vanille; all very good in their way. I confess I like the taste, if it is not talked about. There's a refinement in the thing, especially since we have cut our gross joints, and have taken to *diners à la Russe.* Of course I do not prefer a gourmand; 'I like only an epicure; and the superintendence of such matters should be left to the mistress and the cook. I would as soon see a man hopelessly drunk, as hear him talk about eating.

Bentley was a sub in a marching regiment, at which dignity he had arrived with some difficulty. He was not by any means at the top of the tree either; still he thought it desirable to cultivate an acquaintance with made dishes, and he could scarcely have had a better opportunity than at the pastrycook's shop, over which he resided. Had he had a natural taste for this sort of thing, he might have attained to a knowledge of culinary smells. The odours which were wafted from below to the ensign's quarters, if not always pleasant, were appetising and various. Mr. Oldham supplied half Leamington with dinners and suppers; and if he couldn't do for an ensign and his friends, it was a pity.

But Ensign Bentley was not to be put off with rechauffés. "Crambe repetita" was not to his taste. He was out to see the world; and metaphorically he still wore his hat slightly on one side, and carried a little cane in the pocket of his lounging-coat. He had almost forgotten his own neighbourhood, where his father kept a moderate pack of hounds in a difficult country, somewhere in the West of England; and had condescended to come to Leamington at that excellent sportsman's expense, who found him two horses, and desired him to see how they did things in the Midland Counties.   Ensign Bentley, or the "Captain," as the maids called the young man at home, had a very good opinion of himself; indeed, he was a great card at Leamington among the ladies, at the Regent, over the billiard-table, and across a counter; so that the dinner to which Frank Beauclerc had victimised himself was not so bad as might have been expected.

Fairfax had been in a dragoon regiment : was of a certain age : had long sold out; but retained a cheerful bowing or hail-fellow-well-met sort of acquaintance with the whole of the British Army. If he had any better dinner or company in prospect than that of Bentley, he would not have been there ; as it was, his virtue was rewarded by meeting Frank Beauclerc, whom he already knew and esteemed ; and the good opinion of such a valuable public servant ought to have been highly flattering to our hero.

"What do you drink, Beauclerc ? " said Bentley,

with the aplomb of a general officer on a volunteer
review-day.

" Claret, if you please. Just put it before the
fire a moment." He did so.

Fairfax was warming his in his hand.

" What brought you to this place, Bentley? I
thought you were bound to whip in to your governor, if you got leave," said Frank.

" Oh! no man alive could stand that country.
Besides, the governor took to mounting me on the
servants' horses at last. Impossible to stand that,
you know."

" I suppose not; there's a great difference between the value of a good huntsman and an ensign
in the Hundred and Ninety-first." Bentley had an
idea he was being chaffed, but he only laughed and
helped himself to the claret.

" And who is there here?" said Frank, again.
" Any one I know?"

" Let's see: there's General Blazer and the
girls, and Fred Bubbleton and old Sir Patrick
Macfussell and his niece. You recollect the Mac-

fussells, Beauclerc? they had that house on the
Portbridge road, on the right-hand side out of
Lymmersfield." Frank looked oblivious. He
hadn't got to his point yet; but he drank on in
hope of doing so.

"Don't you recollect they used to sit just in
front of the Mannings in church; a girl with red
eyes and brown hair—no—I mean brown eyes
and red hair?" No; Frank had forgotten her;
such beauty had not made an impression, or he
was preoccupied. At last it came.

"Oh! and, Beauclerc, who do you think was at
the hospital ball the other night? Why, Violet
Carloss and Madame Rosenfels."

"Really: and what had she to say for herself?"

"Why, she asked after our fellows, you know.
I think she mentioned you." Frank felt savage.
"No, now I think of it, I remember she did
not." Frank thought this a bad sign; in reality it
was a good one. But then he was inexperienced
in the ways of woman. "But Fairfax can tell

you more about her than I can. He danced half a dozen times with her while she was here; it's more in his way;" and here the junior ensign spread out his feet before the fire, and assumed a man-of-the-world sort of look, which suited remarkably ill with short light hair of the regulation cut, and the smallest *soupçon* of down on his upper lip. Frank turned to Fairfax, who said:

"What! do you know the Carloss? By Jove, what a beautiful girl! What eyelashes they are, to be sure. What an odd thing, too, we were talking about your fellows; she knows Tom Dashwood and Charlie Ryder, and one or two others. The old woman kept a pretty sharp look-out; wouldn't have 'em at any price, I can tell you. That fellow Dashwood was going it tremendously."

"Was he? Not a bad fellow, Dashwood!" Frank was forced to say something.

"No; and he'll be old Tremencourt's heir: I shouldn't wonder if there's something up in that quarter. She'd never be such a fool as to refuse him. She shut up young Lionel Cotton, the Manchester swell, most splendidly. He was awfully sweet on her: and he thinks nobody can say 'no' to eighteen thousand a year." Beauclerc was getting interested.

"Ah! how was that?" Frank lit a cigar, and smoked rather savagely.

"Well, he's a way of staring, you know; I don't think he means anything, but he's a deuce of a fellow to stare, you know."

"Confound his impudence," said Frank, biting the end of one of Mr. Carlin's very best regalias, at four guineas a pound.

"Ah! he's not a bad fellow, though; but, I suppose, she didn't like it, and said, 'I hope you'll know me again, Mr. Cotton.' Deuced cool, wasn't it?"

"Rather so," said Bentley. Frank said nothing: but he knew pretty well how she would have said it, unless she was much altered.

"So Cotton said, 'I'm sure I may ask the same question, Miss Carloss?'"

"Did he? I wish I'd been behind him."

"Yes he did; and what do you think she said? Why, she said, 'Yes, Mr. Cotton, and I'll answer it. I hope you'll be so much improved in your manners that I shan't know you at all.' Cotton shut up for an hour or two. But I think it's a pretty clear case with Tom Dashwood."

The conversation then took a general turn. Fairfax was very communicative, and tolerably well up in Leamington scandals. Frank was not sorry when the time came to wish them good night: which he did in the middle of an interesting narrative of "*une femme comprise*," a foreign Marchioness who was supposed to be pining from an unrequited attachment to Mr. Fairfax himself.

After breakfast the next morning he went on leave for four or five days, and by dinner-time he was at Lymmersfield: a sudden recognition of his obligations towards his old tutor and his tutor's wife suggested the visit before his change of quarters.

They were delighted to see him—who ever was not?—and he dined heartily on something plainer

but not less excellent than *Salmi aux perdrix*
and *champagne!* He did ample justice to the
South Down mutton and Burgundy, which his old
tutor put before him. He had asked after pretty
nearly everybody in the village, but he had not yet
mustered courage to inquire for Violet.

"Why shouldn't I?" thought he: but he never
did. At last Colville left the room; and while
Mrs. Colville worked away at an antimacassar, he
ventured to inquire for her. Men are always
bolder with women on such subjects.

"I thought you'd forgotten her quite, Frank.
It's such a time since you were here."

"Forgotten her; oh no! Certainly not that
—only—only—you see—I——" here he stuck
fast, and Mrs. Colville did not come to the rescue.
She continued her crochet-work, and looked pro-
vokingly quiet and handsome. She thought Frank
was capricious, and it disappointed her.

"I suppose I shall see her to-morrow," added he,
making the remark in as common-place a tone of
voice as he well could.

"I suppose not, Frank. They came home

the day before yesterday, and went to Brighton
this afternoon. Madame has let her house
again."

"Brighton!" Then the mischief was out : and
they were gone down at Tom Dashwood's sugges-
tion. He forgot that Tom didn't know the route
the last time he could have seen her. It wasn't
out till the day after. He swallowed his tea spas-
modically : and then began to think with a book
before him. Four days in this confounded place
without her!

The next day he borrowed Colville's hack. I
am not romantic myself, but I can forgive Frank
for having ridden round the bank of the lake from
which he had helped to rescue poor Violet. Surely
she couldn't have forgotten him!

And what did Frank in his solitary ride?
Well, he thought not very kindly of that ass
Dashwood. Then he wondered whether it would
not have been as well that the waters of the lake
had closed over them both for ever. But he was
just enough to know that this world is not so rich in

loveliness and innocence as to have easily spared
Violet. "To die old is only to separate for a short
time; to be separated young is to die indeed."
Frank was half a sentimentalist, for which I like
him: but he was a man of action, too, for which I
like him still better. There and then he determined to play out the game, and to go with his
regiment to Brighton.

In the mean time dinner awaited him at Lymmersfield. Heaven knows, he cared nothing about
dinner that day. But Mrs. Colville was a friend in
need, and it was a comfort to have some one to
whom to open his heart: and when she saw the
wound, surely she could pour in oil and wine.

"Frank, you're not happy," said that lady after
dinner on that day, when Colville had retired
to his study. "Can I be of any service to
you?"

Indeed she could, of the greatest, and he told
her so.

"Mrs. Colville, you think me very odd, I dare
say?"

"Not at all. Only as capricious as other people, which I did not think you."

"Then help me out of a difficulty. I've been to the lake at St. Hilda's."

" So I should have guessed, and a less far-sighted person might have done so."

" Indeed, why so ?" and Frank looked eagerly for a solution which would have saved him an explanation.

"Because I saw Harry's pony's legs were adorned with the red clay peculiar to that district." This was scarcely the answer he expected.

" Now you're laughing at me."

"And do you not deserve it? Violet Carloss has been round that lake fifty times to your once. Now you must make a confidante of me."

"Ah! you guess my secret, I see."

" It ought to be no secret, unless she shares it with you. I can't tell how that may be." Was this not justifiable fishing under the circumstances ?

" You know, I've had so few opportunities."

s 2

"Opportunities are made by sensible men. There! don't go," for Frank exhibited some signs of retreating.   And before Colville rejoined them, he made up his mind to go to Brighton.   Women are the best doctors for heart-complaint.

CHAPTER XIV.

A TRANSPLANTATION.

Cœlum, non animum, mutant qui trans mare currunt.—Hor.

EVERARD BEAUCLERC, the father of Frank, was a remarkable-looking man at the time we speak of. He was remarkably handsome in the first place. He was pale, without being sallow, which latter many of our Indian officers and civilians are after a lengthened sojourn in that climate. He was scarcely to be called dark. His hair was brown and unchanged in colour. His eyes were grey, but the length and colour of the lashes gave them a depth and earnestness which they might otherwise have wanted. His nose was straight and well formed, and his mouth rather full, but with handsome and regular teeth, which he showed when he smiled. He wore a long and drooping moustache, without beard; and his whiskers were thin and straight in line, but wavy and silken in substance. In fact, his face had that clean European look which was successfully achieved by cavalry officers of a past date. He was slight and tall, fully six feet high: but his shoulders were broad and flat, and his figure sloped gracefully down, triangularly, to his feet, giving his flanks that unmistakable promise of joint activity and strength so peculiarly English. He was really forty-five years of age, with an appearance at least ten years younger.

He often smiled, whether to show his teeth or his disposition I cannot tell: probably, from both causes. His friends had rarely seen him out of temper, his acquaintances never.

To physiognomists his face was pre-eminently that of one who never said "No" to himself or others. He was self-indulgent, and facile of temper; a not unfrequent combination, though, at first sight, somewhat anomalous. There was talent, too, in his broad white forehead, and courage; but it was rather the courage of impulse and physique than that of stern self-reliance and high principle. Generous he was, for it was painful to him to be otherwise : and he was not indifferent to the reputation which is acquired by occasional great sacrifices at the expense of many petty negligences of that virtue.

It is a great thing to be able to say "No" in the right place. It entails a victory over self, which is far greater than a victory over many cities. Colonel Beauclerc had never attained to that degree of generalship. He had had his moments of good resolution, but had always capitulated when the enemy presented himself in a specious form. He was too fond of treating resolution, and his resolution never rejected the bribe.

It must not be inferred from this that Everard Beauclerc was a dishonourable man. Nothing of the sort. He would have fought a duel, had it lain in his way, as Falstaff would have picked up honour. He could not have said, "No." He would have paid a debt, if he had stripped himself of his last farthing, for he could not have said "No." But then the creditor must have presented himself as the first claimant, or the farthing would have gone in charity or a cheroot. He would not have defrauded his neighbour of a pleasure, an appointment, a rupee; but he would not have been equally particular about his wife : always provided that she was handsome, weak, and had fallen in his way. He could scarcely be called actively vicious ; for he never jumped the rails which hedges in virtue while the ordinary road was open to him and equally pleasant. This disposition gives a man false notions of honour and honesty, and the world is apt to endorse the bill which he draws upon it at sight.

He had been brought up in a school calculated to encourage, or rather not to restrain, the vices of a haughty and chivalrous temperament, not to stimulate its virtues. He had been taught to make the world his idol. Like many men of naturally good feelings, he worshipped it with a divided worship—the worship rather of habit than of heart. I think if he had been blessed with a snub nose, bad teeth, and a large stomach, and had been early marked with the small-pox, he would have been a good man. As it was, he was a singularly popular one, with faults that never impeded his advancement.

When he was young, religion in schools meant one of two things: a lofty aspiration beyond the intelligence of boyhood, and quite impracticable amongst its duties and its pleasures; or an ultra-asceticism sure to be condemned and kicked at by high spirits and fashionable scholarship. The consequence was a moderate indifference, which laughed at nothing and cared for nothing. It pervaded masters as well as boys; and all that was good and great vacillated between a Pericles and a Plato. He went to church and said his prayers to please his mother; but his firmest belief was in his talent for short whist and his high connexions.

Frank was, in many respects, like his father;

but that blank paper, of which philosophers speak, had been early impressed in a better school. He had had the opportunity of learning that boys should be honourable from some higher motive than high birth; that there were more kinds of courage than one, and more principles of action than position in society. He had been taught this from his earliest years, and had seen it acted upon by Dr. Armstrong and those in whom he reposed confidence. The curse of former public education in fashionable society was this: that men became good in spite of false premises, or taxed all their energies only to become great.

Everard Beauclerc sat in the verandah of a handsome house in that city of palaces, Calcutta. It was detached, built of brick, and stuccoed. It looked towards the north. It was not hot, but the air was soft and mild, and the Colonel smoked his cheroot and thought of many things. The ground story was unused, and he occasionally listened to hear the sound of wheels which might enter the spacious porte cochère beneath the pillared porch and covered yard, which belonged to the basement of his house. He watched the craft on the river, here a rapid stream of a mile broad, with the steamers paddling up to the quay. The busy hum of voices came to him with the soft sea breeze, and the sounds of the life that passed to and fro on the "Course" was borne to him with a pleasant murmur.

At present he waited for his friend Mr. Finney, the junior partner in a great banking firm in Calcutta. He arrived at last; an hour after his time. The flush of business was upon his brow as he stepped out of his carriage and came up-stairs.

"My dear Colonel, I am come in person to answer your note, as I told you I would."

Mr. Finney's person was not such as one would have desired especially to have come. However, here he was, and as the business was important, and the Colonel merely offered him a seat in the verandah and a cheroot, we need say no more about it.

"Thank you, Finney; it's very good of you to come. I really feel quite a lassitude. I suppose it's this confounded climate."

"No one ought to be less hard upon it than you. You look as young as you did twenty years ago."

Finney was a cunning-looking person, small-eyed, long-nosed, with a serpent-like figure that might have penetrated and coiled itself round the profoundest depths of a man's heart. His object at present was to fascinate: it was his worst point. So he smoked the Colonel's cheroot, notwithstanding that it made him a little uncomfortable.

"Do I really, Finney? I don't feel so."

"You do, indeed. The climate agrees with you wonderfully. You ought to stop out here and become a millionnaire."

"A mummy you mean, my good fellow. No, no; I've arranged my affairs, and, as I said, I must realise. I've put the business into Sharker and Flint's hands, and they must see me through it."

Sharker and Flint were just the people that

Mr. Finney did not care to recognise in the Colonel's affairs just then.

"You might be a millionnaire a few years hence, Beauclerc—a millionnaire, and still a young man." Finney rubbed his nose thoughtfully.

"A millionnaire without a liver is not so good as a goose with one."

"And after all," continued the financier, appearing to commune with himself, but aloud, "what a pittance in England is a few thousands a year to a man of such taste, such refinement, such capabilities for enjoyment, such——"

"That's just the reason. I want to go while I have those capabilities of enjoyment, and not when I'm dried up, worn out, and miserable. Besides, you're such a nabob, my dear Finney. What's your idea of a pittance? You bankers must have had a fine time of it."

"Indeed we have; and that's why I should recommend you to think twice before you draw your money out of the Anglo-Banian Bank. One hundred and fifty-three thousand pounds will be found to be something less than one million one hundred and fifty-three thousand rupees."

" Let's call it a hundred and fifty."

" Let's call it what it is. Your friends Sharker and Flint will, I can tell you."

" Well, it's enough to live upon, at all events."

" Not as you live. Let me see. At three per cent., with the funds at par, that will be just four thousand——"

" There, never mind that : have another cheroot."

" On no account; no, thank you," said Finney, who was more at home with his Colenso than his tobacco; "on no account. But, as I was saying, four thousand five hundred a year is no great income to begin upon in England. To be sure, there's your uncle's estate, which may be worth——"

" The Jews have had the best part of it long ago. It's let on a lease, or I'd go and live at the place myself, and take the hounds."

" Take the hounds !" said old Finney, with

a stare, his own profligacy lying quite in a different direction to dogs and horses.

"Yes; why not? I suppose I'm not so infirm yet as not to be able to ride."

"Oh! it's not the riding, it's the money I'm thinking of."

"You don't mean to say that a man with a hundred and fifty thousand pounds and a place in the country, which must produce something, can't be master of a pack of fox-hounds?"

"I know nothing about hounds; but I should think not, when he only gets three per cent. for it. We've allowed you seven, and you have contrived occasionally to overdraw."

There is no denying the facts of Mr. Finney, nor the extravagance of the Colonel's life, who would have managed to spend any sum of money that could be placed at his disposal. In a capital remarkable for its luxuries and waste, Everard Beauclerc was running the wealthiest Europeans or natives close for first place.

The Colonel understood the position in which

Finney's statistics had placed him, and meditated, probably as much as he ever had meditated, about money matters.   Mr. Finney pushed his advances. " And you give up your appointment, too, and retire upon half-pay ?"

" Of course ;" and the Colonel pulled his moustache into his mouth, and held the end of it between his lips, with him an unfailing sign of profundity.

" Why not leave the money, if you must go, and draw upon us for your income at sight ? Nothing easier : a thing done every day."

" Do you remember me when I first married : three or four and twenty years ago ? I was very young, and married imprudently, people said. They said so in England : but I didn't think so. Well ! I had thirty thousand pounds then, only— it wasn't much, to be sure—but it was all ; and it was in the hands of one of your great houses : Snatchem's. I didn't get much of it back, as you may suppose."

" Three shillings in the pound," said Finney,

with a pious ejaculation on the wickedness of mankind in general and bankers in particular. "After all, they were but adventurers from Liverpool or Manchester."

"I did not ask what they were; but I woke one fine morning, and went out shooting with Jennyns and Goldicott. They didn't know that I had anything to do with it; but mentioned the failure at luncheon. It was only for two millions three hundred thousand. That was a trifle after Alexander's, you know."

"What *did* you do?" said old Finney, wondering in his own mind what his friend would do if he had just now such a pleasant piece of intelligence to announce.

"Well! it rather upset me, and I missed the first small deer after tiffin; but it made me dreadfully savage; and in the afternoon I shot a tiger, and won fourteen hundred of Bungalow at écarté. One can't do much with fourteen hundred; but it's better than nothing."

Mr. Finney thought it was. "Those were awk-

ward times for young men. The merchants and
bankers were most improvident, reckless in their
way of trading. They speculated in all sorts of
things."

" Speculated!" said Beauclerc, regarding the
loss at a distance as rather a joke, " I believe you;
I don't know what I was not a holder of. Indigo,
silk, cotton, raw sugars—what the d—l are they?—
and monkey-skins; and then down they came upon
us. I don't think Snatchem was much the worse
for it. He sold his race-horses; but he continued
to live and give dinners, much as usual. I
remember his horses, for I bought one of 'em
myself: ' a thorough-bred one, by the King of
Oude.' "

Finney opened his eyes at this very singular
mode of retrenchment. "I gave a hundred sovereigns for him, and won the Nizam's Cup, worth
at least two thousand rupees, and about twenty
thousand more in bets; so that spec answered
better than raw sugar and monkeys' tails, you
see."

" Yours has been a curious life, Colonel. However, you're pretty safe now."

" By Jove! I hope so. When my uncle died a few years after, it quite set me up. Ah! poor dear Florence : she didn't live to see it. I've had some lucky *coups* since then. And you think I could do best by leaving the money in your hands ? "

" My dear Colonel, what's the difference between four thousand five hundred and ten thousand five hundred ?"

" Well, you know best, I dare say. It's a good deal of money, as you say."

" And as safe as the Bank of England."

" That's just what they said of Alexander's—and of Snatchem—and the rest of them—but they all came to grief."

" But what a different state of things ! Look at the lives they led ! the extravagance, the immorality, the insane speculation, the gambling——"

" Very likely, Finney ; but you don't mean to say there are no more cakes and ale because Snatchem's gone, and you stand ?"

"There was a general demoralisation of Indian society at the time you speak of, shocking to contemplate;" and the banker looked piously horrified. Everard Beauclerc seemed rather entertained, and replied :

"Yes! to be sure there was : they were no worse than their creditors, at all events, in those respects, you know. To be sure, they added robbery to their abnegation of the rest of the Decalogue; but then it was on a grand scale; and the Bankruptcy Court, like society, pardons vice on a large scale with a magnanimity she never uses towards minor infirmities. Poor old Snatchem! I'm glad he went on again. His son's one of the aides-decamp at Government House."

"Ah! my dear Colonel Beauclerc, you make a joke of everything; you always did; but in those days we lived over a volcano, and when it burst it spread ruin far and wide. Think of the widow and orphan——"

"And of the unhappy subaltern, who got nothing out of it but a hundred-guinea screw——"

"Ha! ha! it's no use talking to you now : we

must have this matter over seriously another time. If we can set you up in England with ten thousand a year, Colonél, with your opportunities you may be anything. You may have all the packs of dogs in Newmarket, and your boy — bless my heart!—you may return him for the county. Think of that: young Frank, member for the county."

This was a chord to which the Colonel always responded. "Well, I suppose it would be a great advantage. I think nothing more need be done in the matter till I see Sharker and Flint."

"D—n Sharker and Flint," said the pious banker as he went down-stairs, and met Captain Jennyns coming up.

"So you really mean going next month, Beauclerc, do you?" said the Captain.

"Well! you see, I had made up my mind, but——"

"So you had three years ago, when your boy was first gazetted. It's more than an even bet you don't go now." And the Captain stroked his moustache.

"Indeed I must. I mean to go; but I want to settle some money matters. There's old Finney; 'pon my soul, I think that fellow's a rascal with that Anglo-Banian bank of his: he's been here, and I've given my lawyers orders to get my account out of his hand, and put everything straight between us."

When Jennyns heard of Mr. Finney's visit and the Anglo-Banian Bank, his face turned a shade paler than usual; and he blew a prolonged whistle.

"Why, what's the matter now?" said the Colonel.

"If it's not impertinent, old fellow, may I ask what you consider the amount of your property of one sort or another in that concern?"

"Yes, you may, Charlie. I've just heard, one hundred and fifty-three thousand pounds some shillings; and what the devil to do with the odd three thousand I'm sure I can't tell."

"Don't let that trouble you; come with me." They were soon in the Captain's carriage, and driving along the Course, where nods and signs of recognition greeted them constantly.

"The sooner you're out of this concern the better for you, Beauclerc. Sharker and Flint are bad enough; but that's a harbour of refuge compared to the Anglo-Banian business."

"I've ordered Sharker to get the affair wound up a month ago." The Colonel did not say that he had just been about rescinding the order. That sort of reticence was so like him.

"We'll stir up old Sharker at once, then. I don't like your Anglo-Indian friends. Report just now doesn't speak highly of them."

"Why, you don't mean to say——"

"I don't mean to say anything; but we'll go and see how matters stand;" and they were soon in the office of Messrs. Sharker and Flint. Sharker was enjoying himself in the cool of the day. Flint was at home. A sharp, hard-featured little man, who looked a match for any number of cavalry officers, and a banker into the bargain.

"Well, Flint, what have you done about my business?"

"What, Mr. Finney and the banking concern! Why, he's just gone; came here to rescind the

order for transmission to England; but we want
your signature to the power of attorney, before
we can do anything." Finney had lost no time.

" How soon can the business be settled?" said
Jennyns, who was a good-looking, wiry sort of
man, with a quick imperious manner, highly au-
thoritative when backed by money and right.

" As soon as the Colonel likes; now, if he pleases;
but if he's going to rescind the order, it doesn't
signify. No importance at all. We'll stop the
proceedings, and the thing can stand over till the
next board day."

" Let's have the papers, and draw out the form.
The Colonel has made up his mind, so we'll sign
at once." Mr. Flint went to a strong-box, whence
he drew forth the lengthiest document on record,
which he proceeded to read. Having finished, he
produced a pen and ink, and, pointing to a favoured
spot, desired the Colonel to sign, seal, and deliver.

In half an hour the Colonel and his friend were
on their way back. The business was to be con-
cluded by that time to-morrow; and when Captain

Jennyns shook hands with his friend, he felt as if he had done a good day's work.

"You're safe enough now, Beauclerc; and about the time you get your first dividend from the Bank of England, you'll read of the failure of a few more Indian houses, and our friend Finney's will be among the first of them."

"You don't mean that?" replied Beauclerc, looking remarkably blue. His friend did mean it, and the Colonel's sleep that night was not so wholesome as it was six weeks later, when the proper course had been adopted, and the transmission of one hundred and fifty thousand pounds into English securities was *un fait accompli*.

We may as well finish up Finney and the Anglo-Banian Company at once. Their failure took place within the twelve months. The Colonel's withdrawal was the first stone which hit the windows of a dilapidated house. They carried on, however, for some time. At length Finney became supernaturally pious, and his coadjutors more luxurious and immoral than usual. A great crash came. Half a dozen houses divided the loss of about fifteen millions between them. Widows and orphans wept, and went into servitude; subalterns and old general officers cursed and drank sangaree, and began life again. Finney forswore champagne and the pleasures of the table for six months; and the confiding public divided five shillings in the pound among them. It would have made a hole in the hundred and fifty thousand.

END OF VOL. I.

LONDON:
PRINTED BY C. WHITING, BEAUFORT HOUSE, STRAND.

www.ingramcontent.com/pod-product-compliance
Lightning Source LLC
Chambersburg PA
CBHW030624030726
47497CB00006B/1628